MRS SMITH'S SUSPECTS
CLAUDE, GORD, ALICE, & MAUD

JINNY ALEXANDER

ISBN Paperback: 978-1-916814-08-0

ISBN Large Print Paperback: 978-1-916814-10-3

ISBN ebook: 978-1-916814-09-7

ISBN Audiobook: 978-1-916814-11-0

Cover Design: Wicked Good Book Covers (www.wickedgoodbookcovers.com)
Cover and title page artwork: Ailee (www.instagram.com/aileemarie_art)
High Street drawing of Little Wittering: Jinny Alexander
Photo of Amber from Jinny's parents' wedding album

Visit www.jinnyalexander.com

This book, and all that follow in this series, are in memory of my grandmother, Jean Alexander (29th July 1921 – 10th October 1979), and her guide dog, Amber.
I have only a handful of memories of this grandma, but through Mrs Smith and Amity, those scant memories live on.

AMBER 1970

Thank you also to Emily Trapp, who suggested the name 'Amity' for Mrs Smith's guide dog. It's the perfect name!

A note to my American-English readers

I'm so glad you're here! I'm a British author, living in the Republic of Ireland, and all my books are set in Ireland or the UK. As such, I use British English in my writing so you'll notice a few extra letters – Us after Os, for instance, and Ls that come in pairs. I make up for these extras by using fewer Zs...

I hope you'll enjoy my natural English voice and immerse yourselves fully into my UK and Irish settings and characters, but if you're still not convinced, I recommend a nice cup of tea.

Over here, a nice cup of tea fixes almost everything.

Love, Jinny xx

Little Wittering High Street

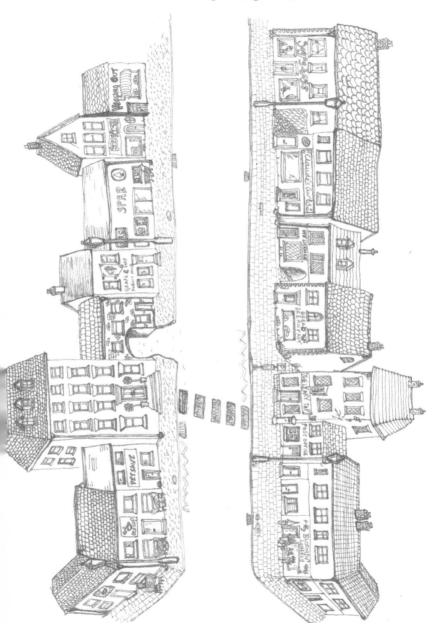

Chapter One

On account of Robert J. Robertson lying dead in the broom cupboard, Dennis and I were going to be terribly late with dinner.

By the time P.C. Doofus Finbury arrived at Claude's Curls hairdressing salon, the body was stiffening and I was sipping as daintily as anyone could from a thick earthenware mug with a handle that even my twig-thin fingers could barely fit through, clearly designed by an idiot. I craved a proper cup of Earl Grey, brewed in a teapot and left to stand for sufficient time, poured through a strainer into my Royal Albert with the matching milk jug, all covered in flowers I can no longer see.

My feeble attempts at manoeuvring the monstrosity were interrupted by Doofus Finbury, who has no understanding of personal space. I reeled backwards as a waft of Marlboro cigarettes and something I strongly suspected was the remainder of a sausage sandwich smacked me in the face. I knew it was Doofus Finbury, not from the smell—anyone can smell of sausage sandwich on certain days—but from his shrill, boyish voice and the way he bandied a delusional air of jumped-up authority.

"And, why, Mrs Smith," he demanded, up close and personal, "did you think it a *good* idea to poke the corpse with the end of your cane?"

I lowered the brick-heavy mug onto my lap and answered him in my sweetest voice. "I may have accidentally rested the end of my cane on the poor man, you silly little boy, because if I were able to see where I was placing the end of my cane, it would be entirely unnecessary for me to use a cane." I may have tutted, just a little, but the infuriating man is quite as insufferable and lacking in his faculties as he was as a spotty fourteen-year-old boy in the back row of my fourth-year English classes fifteen years ago. That he was accepted into the police force is an occurrence that leaves me frequently flummoxed.

Finbury huffed and I expect he opened and closed his mouth like a fish for a moment or two, as he loitered wordlessly beside my chair, in a literal embodiment of one who hangs around like a bad smell. Mercifully, before managing to form any further imbecilic sentences, he was called away by dear Claude. I suspected dear Claude had no more desire to speak with the idiot child than I, but needs must when somebody is lying dead in one's cleaning cupboard.

Left untended in my salon chair, I took up the blessed mug and tried to make the best of things, in the hope that I would not be entirely parched whilst awaiting permission to leave Claude's Curls.

Before we go any further, I must confess that the buffoon's name is not, as a matter of fact, Doofus Finbury, but Dougal Rufus Finbury, just as my own name is not, of course, Salamander Smith. No one is *christened* Salamander. My name is Sally Amanda Smith, so you can see, I imagine, why it might be that Dennis—Dennis is my husband—combined my names in jest, one rainy afternoon sometime roundabout the early nineteen-seventies. From the moment he started it, the name stuck, and while I do not object to it from my closest friends, you may refer to me as Mrs Smith.

Regardless, I needed to be rid of that blessed mug, before the weight of it caused permanent damage to my wrist, so I'm sorry to say I waved it around in much the manner of one seeking a passing waiter, and called out to anyone near enough to be of assistance, "If somebody would care to relieve me of this mug, I would very much like to be on my way."

To my great relief, the voice that answered was that of dear Claude. The air around me swished, and the heady fragrance of Dior Sauvage preceded the hand that plucked the mug from my grasp and set it, with a clunk, onto the shelf in front of me.

"I don't think you're allowed to leave just yet, Mrs S. They still need to ask a few more questions. You just sit there and relax and try not to worry."

He sounded worried. *Pot, kettle.* I tutted, but kept the thought to myself.

Claude's bulky frame shifted sideways, and beyond him, more fuzzy shadows bustled and swore.

"Sit there," he'd said.

I wasn't having that.

It is not sensible for one of my advanced years to remain still for a prolonged amount of time. It is one thing to have given up my own hips a decade or so ago, and quite another to allow the artificial ones to lock up. At least, that is the story I would have spun if anyone had attempted to stop me. I pulled myself to my feet with a firm grasp of the faux-leather arms of the chair, and groped for the offending cane.

"If that is the case," I told dear Claude, "I will need to visit the ladies' room again. I trust *that* will be allowed."

Not very long after his arrival on the scene, Doofus Finbury had done his utmost to confiscate my white stick as evidence. I can, of course, manage well enough without my cane when accompanied by Amity, but for visits to the salon, it is kinder and more practical to leave her at home with Dennis. I suspect he is grateful of the company, when I am absent, although he is unlikely to admit it. Amity, I am certain, is grateful for any opportunity to behave as a normal dog, off-duty for a few blissful hours. Dennis will throw a ball for her in the garden, as long as it doesn't rain, and she will gleefully play fetch until one of them tires. Nonetheless, in the hair salon, I *do* need my cane, so when Finbury attempted to take it, I had cited my rights and quoted imaginary legal cases plucked from the air. The little gimlet had lapped it up; quaked in his too-tight boots, and handed me the cane with a stuttering warning about watching where I put it.

"You flibbert." I'd told him, pinning him with what I hoped was a fearsome gaze, despite no longer being able to gaze at anything with any degree of success. "If I could watch where I was putting it—"

"I ... I ..." He had cut me off with an inconsequential stammer, and I suspected that as he hastily retreated on squeaking footsteps, his face was a red as a bloody Mary. Something of which I would happily avail if only anyone would think to offer any of us anything stronger than an overly milky mug of entirely unpalatable own-brand tea.

"So," I repeated to darling Claude, "I will just make my way to the ladies' room, and then, if you would be so kind, I would very much appreciate a *proper* cup of tea in a vessel that does not double as a small lifeboat." I retrieved my cane from where I had safely stashed it out of Finbury's reach, between my leg and the side of the chair, and tap-tapped my way across the salon on the pretence of heading to the lavatories for the second time that afternoon.

There are many ways to distinguish between a cleaning cupboard and a lavatory, and in Claude's Curls hairdressing salon, the key difference is that the cleaning cupboard smells strongly of bleaches and perming solutions, and the lavatories emit a distinct whiff of stale urine, lemon toilet duck, and vanilla; the latter a determined attempt to mask the former. Unfortunately, on this particular afternoon, as of sometime yet undetermined, the cleaning cupboard also smelled of urine, entirely unmasked by vanilla, and the metallic tang of blood.

It was this pungent yet misplaced odour of stale urine that had brought the matter to my attention, twenty minutes or so before Finbury's arrival, and caused me to hesitate momentarily, unsure whether I had lost my bearings.

I had, a few moments before that point, been sitting perfectly still, listening to that lovely Richard Osman's murder book on the clever reading device on my telephone contraption, with my head entirely covered in foil as if I were some kind of conspiracy theorist.

The persistent waft of ammonia had caused my eyes to water, and I had been grateful I could listen perfectly well to my book unhindered by the prickling tears. There are *some* small mercies in becoming almost blind, although many of them are assisted considerably by some rather splendid advancements of technology and would not have been at all possible in my grandmother's day, so I was grateful for that, at least, on the days on which I found myself feeling a little sorry for myself. The ability to listen to a delightful voice emanating from within my telephone, reading aloud to me in a hair salon, is one such merciful invention (once you discount the obvious interruptions necessitated by the brandishing of scissors in the vicinity of one's ears).

Much as I was enjoying that lovely Richard Osman, at my age, it takes little to trigger a desire to visit the ladies', and the mere *thought* of my watering eyes soon developed into a more pressing waterworks problem. A small snicker at a witty comment in the story sealed the fate of my bladder. By the time I tapped my way to the ladies', I had become accustomed to the ammonia but was in urgent need of relieving myself in other departments.

This is how, as I attempted to inform that imbecile, Doofus Finbury, I can be totally confident of the time of discovery. Of the corpse, that is.

Alice had announced the time quite clearly as I had heaved myself from my seat. "Yes, go now," she'd said in that breathy, Marilyn Monroe little-girl's voice. Alice is my usual colourist, and although she was just as ditsy as always that day, I have become quite fond of her. Claude took her on some years ago, as a favour to Maud, but she is proving quite capable, if you excuse her tendency to drop things. She had already dropped a hairbrush, a spatula, two hair clips, and several drips of hair dye, before we even got to the unfortunate discovery of the corpse, which even for Alice, seemed an excessive amount of flustering so I suspected she'd had a busy day and was looking forward to having a few days off over the festive period. She likes to give a commentary as she works, so she tells me what she drops, which is thoughtful, although I usually tune her out, much as one tends to do with Radio Four when doing household chores.

"Two-thirty-six," she'd said, as I'd started to get up. "We've another thirty-five minutes before we can take this off. I'd say you're ready to stretch your legs." She'd passed me my cane, turned me gently around to face the direction of the lavatories, and bustled away to attend to someone else.

I did not, of course, intervene, when I first noticed the unfortunate smell emanating from the cleaning cupboard. I merely took a moment to gather myself, and determined I was still several steps short of the ladies'. It was on my return journey, no longer distracted by the need to urinate, that I faltered once more on the threshold of the cupboard. The smell was still present so I pushed open the door and tentatively tapped my cane around the floor, hoping to establish the cause of the offending odour.

The shape on the floor was a mere shadow; a dark mound against a light floor. I am just about able to make out shadow and light, but it is as if one is watching the world through a steamed-up car window on a foggy evening in winter, with the world defined only as fuzzy white frost clinging to dark edges. There is no colour. I do so miss colours.

My cane met some resistance, although the shape, as I prodded it, was soft and pliant. The smell, now the door was open, was layered and pungent. The usual array of chemicals vied for attention, and whilst ammonia was dominant, you will agree that the ammonia from hair products is marginally more palatable than the ammonia of stale urine. I was fairly certain I could distinguish both, but perhaps the odour from the lavatories was lingering in my nostrils, as it sometimes does. I concluded that the soft shadowy shape must be a bundle of soiled towels, and returned to my seat. Once I had settled myself as comfortably as these chairs allow, and set my feet on that neat little footrest one finds attached to the underside, I suggested to Alice that she may wish to remove the pile of offending towels in the cupboard to a more distant vicinity.

"There is," I said, keeping my voice low so as not to disturb Claude's other clients with such an unsavoury matter, "a remarkably unpleasant aroma therein."

Alice, her hand resting on my shoulder, gave a little shudder that rustled the foils in my hair, but she is compliant and willing and eager to please, so she went to investigate.

Thus it was that one minute I was sitting back in the styling chair, my head still wrapped like a turkey dinner in strips of foil, and that lovely Richard Osman reinstated in my earphones; the next, Alice's shrill screams pierced the air.

From that moment, the salon descended into a frenzy that I witnessed as a blur of movement; a frisson of shifting air, and an awful lot of high-pitched indecision.

"Is he ..."

"Don't touch him!"

"Take his pulse!"

"See if he's breathing!"

"Put him in the recovery position."

"Don't move him!"

Until at last, darling Claude's deep, level voice rose above them all. "Phone the police."

The movement stilled, and silence fell into the empty space following Claude's firm instruction.

The silence lasted for approximately seven seconds before the babble started again.

"Who?"

"What will we tell them?"

"Is he ...?"

"Enough." Claude's voice was louder now, with a finality that told his staff to calm themselves down, pull themselves together, and get a grip. "Alice, Bobby-Jo, get back to your clients before their hair boils. Lily, sweetheart, don't stand there gawping; go and lock the front door, there's a good girl. Flora, call the police. Ask them to come immediately and—" He lowered his voice to a murmur that anyone would have struggled to decipher.

Except me. Fortunately, the hairdryers had stopped as the panic had started, and my hearing, in compensation for my eyesight, is as finely-tuned as my sense of smell.

"Tell them," Claude whispered, from somewhere behind me, in the vicinity of the lavatories, "that there appears to be a dead man in our cleaning cupboard."

There was another shrill squeal, followed by a thud.

Claude said something I don't care to repeat, and a moment later, after the rapid-fire pushing of telephone buttons at the salon reception desk—*bip, bip, bip*—he spoke to the emergency services himself, in a low, steady baritone.

"Excuse me," I called out, after what I considered to be a reasonable amount of time had passed. "Excuse me, dear Claude. Is everything all right?"

Chapter Two

Of course, I was perfectly aware that everything was *not* all right, and once poor Alice had been helped up from the floor upon which she had fainted, and placated with a cup of tea and platitudes which I suspect were of little help, she was instructed by Claude to attend to my hair colour.

You may think Claude unsympathetic, but he is a sensible man and probably wanted to keep the poor girl occupied. Whilst it is also true he would not have wished a client's hair to frizzle, one can't suppose that was his foremost concern at that precise moment.

Alice had protested, and begged quite loudly to be allowed to leave, but by that time, Dougal Rufus Finbury had arrived, and we were all captive.

"No one," Alice sniffed, once she had returned to attend to my hair, "is allowed to leave. Dougal took one look in the cupboard, and called for backup." She poked at my foiled scalp with tremulous fingers. "I almost felt sorry for him."

I was, for once, greatly relieved that I could not see the results of my afternoon at the salon, as I am certain her skills were somewhat lacking due to her trembling fingers and lack of concentration.

Nevertheless, my hair needed to be released from its foil trappings, and Alice babbled and sobbed incoherently as she first unpeeled my hair and then dabbed at stray patches of dye that I suspect stained my temples. She scalded me with the rinsing water, and was uncharacteristically rough as she tousled me dry. In between her sobs and sniffles and the spray of too-hot or too-cold that would have frazzled even Goldilocks, I encouraged her to talk. Often, one finds, the best way to process a shock is to talk it through. Moreover, I couldn't deny my curiosity as to the unfolding chaos, and Alice was best-placed to enlighten me.

Claude, dividing his time between the police and his clients, flitted like a trapped butterfly, never quite settling in one spot for long. "You all right, Mrs S.? Anything I can get you?" he'd say, but scuttle away before I could respond.

I would have been supremely grateful for a proper cup of tea, but Alice, still shaky-handed and stuttering, was not in a state to provide one, and Claude appeared to have quite forgotten his manners amongst all the hoohah. One cannot blame him, of course. It must be most disconcerting for any respectable salon owner to locate a corpse amongst their mops and brooms and packets of hair dye—even for a disrespectable salon owner, one supposes, but Claude, I can assure you, was of the respectable type.

The usual background chatter of the busy hair salon had receded to a subdued murmur, with the exception of Doofus Finbury, who spoke at a volume more suited to a children's playground. He had arrived alone, but quickly and loudly summoned for back up in a most animated way. To be perfectly honest, it was exactly as you may expect from those television shows with crackly radios and quick-fire code words, although I suspect any number of more refined officers of the law would have been entirely more discreet about it.

It cannot have been more than fifteen minutes after his assessment of the scene that a police siren wailed to a stop outside the salon, and following the clip of Flora's shoes and the *click-click* of the key in the lock, the door breezed open and closed with a chilly whoosh of December air.

The new arrivals were, if their voices accurately portray their persons, an older man and a middle-aged woman. I would determine the woman to be older than Finbury, who, despite appearance and manner, is now almost thirty years of age. I can no longer make out his face, of course, but I envisage him much as he looked when I taught him: scruffy hair the colour of a dying mouse; acne one may mistake for a measles rash, and those large metal braces affixed to his teeth. I suppose he no longer wears the braces, but those teenage years left an impression from which I have never quite recovered. To this day I remain unsure whether it was purely coincidental that I retired immediately after my two years as form teacher to that particular cohort of students. But I digress. The newly-arrived woman sounded as if she were a solid, sensible police officer with a no-nonsense manner and clunky shoes. Presumably those lace-up ones that stay secured to the feet should the need arise to run for miles after a petty thief. She smelled of commercial soap and the faintest hint of jasmine. A deodorant or hand cream, no doubt.

Her superior—I did not presume her inferiority due to her gender, but on the irrefutable fact that she referred to him as "boss"—had the raspy tones of a smoker and the shuffling gait of a man well into his sixties. Due for retirement, I shouldn't wonder, and then she will step into his job. God forbid it be Doofus Finbury who is destined to fill his shoes, squeaky-clean as Finbury's shoes may be on Claude's usually-spotless salon floor.

Therefore, within fifteen minutes or so since Finbury's arrival, the salon was brimming with bodies. Live ones, that is, except for the obvious. The constant bustling movements of so many dark shadows was quite disorienting, and despite the momentary stunned silence immediately after Alice had fainted, the noise had resumed and redoubled with the arrival of Finbury's reinforcements. One or two of the dryers had started up, as the stylists did their best to salvage the clients' hairdos, but the predominant noises were Alice's sniffs; Claude's stuttering mix of reassurance and worry; sporadic sobs from various quarters, and Doofus Finbury's high-pitched babble countered by the stern and steady voices of his two sensible colleagues. Besides the three police officers and Claude and Alice, there were the other members of Claude's salon staff; four more clients, and me.

Bobby-Jo is one of the more experienced stylists, and has been with Claude for the past four years. She wears Marc Jacobs' Daisy which clashes with the odour of her hair products. I do not need to be able to see her face to know she wears an excessive amount of lipstick and her skin is unnaturally orange. I call into the salon for a blow-dry every Monday, and she usually reeks of recently-applied tanning lotion that almost disguises the rosy odour of freshly-slicked lipstick. The day of Robert J. Robertson's demise, however, was not a Monday; it was a week before Christmas and

I had booked an appointment for a colour as well as the usual wash-and-blow-dry. It was a chilly, blustery Thursday afternoon, and the aroma of tanning lotion was absent.

In fact, Bobby-Jo only arrived in the salon quite some time after Phyllis and me, and I can be quite certain of that because she said, "I'm back! Did you miss me?" quite loudly to goodness knows who, and then Claude said, "Go on then, show us the pics, but not all the boring ones, just the cute ones of your son as we haven't got all day."

Bobby-Jo had laughed, and said, "Hang on a minute ... Here he is. Second Wise Man. The one in the stripey tea towel, not the orange one with the windmill on."

It must have been at least twenty past one by then, I should think, as I had already had my hair washed and Alice had just settled me back in to my seat ready to be dried off.

Gordon had chipped in to ask if he was the king who took a gift of talcum powder, Ferrero Rocher, or bubble bath, and everyone had a little chuckle about that, and then Alice started up the hair dryer and I didn't hear any more about it so I never did find out which gift Bobby-Jo's little son had delivered to the plastic doll in the cardboard manger in the Primary School's nativity play. Nonetheless, I could imagine the scene perfectly well, because although it's been many years since I was last able to *see* a nativity play, they do tend to be much the same from year to year, wouldn't you agree?

Outside the full-height picture window, the shift of light informed me that by the time Doofus Finbury's reinforcements arrived, night was already closing in.

Alice, having done my second rinse, to tidy me up after the colour, once again blasted my head with the hair-dryer for an interminable amount of time in which I could hear or sense little beyond the roar of warm air.

"That's you done, Mrs Smith," she informed me in a more subdued tone than that she usually applied for the big finale, "but I'm afraid you have to sit there until the cops say you can go. Do you want another cuppa?"

Grateful that the stiffening corpse did not prevent access to the tea-making facilities, I dispatched her with a request for a spoonful of extra sugar, and if at all possible, some form of *sensible* mug from which to drink. Whilst she was gone, Finbury granted permission for me to telephone poor Dennis to inform him of the delay.

"I will call him for you and inform him of the situation," Finbury said loudly, as if I were an imbecile, and pompously, as if his mother had knotted his tie too tightly, although I wouldn't be at all surprised if he still wore one of those funny little child's ties with the elastic rather than one for which anyone actually needed to tie a knot, now I come to think about it.

I informed him in my politest voice that I was quite capable, thank you very much, as the device was trained to recognise my voice, albeit in a most baffling way that I cannot begin to understand.

He seemed quite surprised by this, but he relinquished the device into my outstretched hand and allowed me to instruct the clever little machine to connect itself to my husband's telephone.

Dennis answered on the seventh ring, just as I was starting to worry it might go to his voicemail contraption, so I don't know what he was doing with himself but it wasn't the time to get into that, given the far more pressing matter in hand. I spoke quickly before he could initiate any lengthy chat, and was sparse with the details, not wishing to cause poor Dennis any unnecessary concern. As I was not entirely certain we would be released from our salon-captivity any time soon, I suggested he may like to retrieve one of those handy little M&S ready-meals from the freezer—that nice shepherd's pie he enjoys, perhaps. We keep a small supply for just such emergencies and I was quite sure even Dennis could manage to pop one into the microwave for three minutes.

"Don't forget to remove any foil wrappings and prick the plastic film with a fork," I reminded him. "We don't want a repeat of last time, do we dear?" Dennis is not *accustomed* to cooking by himself, even though he has *tried* on occasion in the years since my vision has diminished.

Usually, we attend to dinner together, with Dennis reading labels and weighing ingredients and suchlike, and me doing the stirring and whatnot, but we take Thursdays off, and Dennis orders us one of those takeaway meals from that nice Kangaroo place that hops around the town delivering whatever one desires. I was certainly not going to let Dennis enjoy that excitement without me. He would just have to wait until Friday for his chicken korma and pilau. I was sure he would manage, even though he is seventy-eight.

I do appear to have digressed somewhat, which is a most unfortunate side effect of old age. So many topics have accumulated over my seventy-four years, it becomes increasingly difficult to recall the most pressing. I attempt to remain youthful at heart, but my arthritic aches and failing vision remind me there is little else of me left that is young, these days.

Where were we? Three police officers (if we are to count the bumbling Finbury as such, otherwise: two police officers and an incompetent). Claude. Claude is the proprietor and head-stylist here at Claude's Curls; a well-reputed establishment of which he is rightfully proud. Alice, who slopped my tea just a little as she set it into my hands, although I was pleased to note she had rustled up an altogether more acceptable mug this time. One of those Dunoon ones, I shouldn't wonder, judging by the shape of it. I was going to ask her to describe the pattern to me, but she was gone again, muttering something about having a quick tea-break of her own. I allowed myself to imagine the mug to be decorated in a pleasing array of water-colour flowers, but for all I know, it could display lurid, neon-coloured cartoonish cats.

Bobby-Jo is a pleasant young thing, despite the tanning lotion.

Flora is the receptionist, and she is new. She answers the phone in Claude's Curls every day, but was incapable of telephoning the police in time of need; an observation I filed away for later it case it was of any importance. Claude took her on in the summer, when Lydia left to have another baby. Pops them out, she does, but this time, she decided she may as well stay at home and mind them. "Cheaper than childcare,

Mrs S.," she'd said, with a tinny chuckle, and I haven't seen her since. Figuratively, I mean. I haven't actually *seen* her since before her oldest was born, so that has been a good ten years or more.

Doctor Hornsby frequently reminds me I am fortunate not to have lost my sight earlier, as is often the case with my condition, but I won't bore you with the details of my medical ailments. I'm surprised *he* can see, at his age—Doctor Hornsby, that is. He should have retired years ago and must be a good few years older than my Dennis, I should think.

I can't imagine why on earth I am telling you about Doctor Hornsby. He wasn't in the salon and I doubt very much that he has ever set foot in the place, although his wife and daughters do pop in from time to time. But no, not Doctor Hornsby. At the time the officers arrived, those of us present in the salon were Claude, Alice, Bobby-Jo, Flora. Me. Three police officers. All of us locked inside Claude's Curls hair salon at approximately three-thirty on the last Thursday before Christmas, and beginning to wonder if we would be permitted to exit in time to cook our turkeys. Or whatever one chooses to eat for Christmas dinner in these modern times. I don't imagine many of these people bother with a turkey, now I think about it. Dennis and I no longer bother, not when there are just the two of us and neither of us with the strength to lift a bird of that proportion.

Gordon was there too, of course. Another of the stylists, and Claude's partner in every sense of the word. Gordon is perfectly pleasant and gentlemanly, in a quieter way than Claude, who is what one may very well call *exuberant*. And Lily, who is not exuberant by any means, and is a student, although whether she is a hairdressing student or from the secondary school, Alice wasn't quite clear. She was better with telling me the names of the clients than the details of her co-workers, which I thought was a little unprofessional to tell the truth, but a sure sign of Alice's dizziness, nevertheless. She does like to chatter, and I don't think it's just to indulge my lack of ability to see things for myself. Alice was all of a flutter even before opening the cleaning cupboard door and discovering a corpse, to be perfectly frank, but that's Alice for you.

So that's the stylists and Flora, who isn't a stylist by any stretch of imagination but I suppose she's important to the general running of the place.

Phyllis always collects me when we come to the salon, which allays my need for Amity, of course. We like to come together; make an afternoon of it, with tea in the café or hotel after, or a walk in the park, in summer. With Phyllis escorting me to the salon and home again, and helping me navigate if she deems it necessary, there's really no need at all for Amity to come along and she does so hate the scents in the salon. She's quite professional, despite being young, but the poor animal simply can't help sneezing when all the salon chemicals get up her nose. Phyllis and I are dear friends. She was sat in the opposite seat, behind the mirror-divider. I could hear her chatting to Claude and Bobby-Jo from time to time when the buzz of the salon was quiet enough.

Maud was seated along from Phyllis, nearer to the sinks than Phyllis or me. I'd known Maud was in the salon as soon as I set foot in the door. Alice usually greets me and helps me to my seat, but on that day, she called to me from the waiting area with the information that she would be with me in a minute, she was just getting her gran a cup of tea, and Maud is Alice's grandmother, so it wasn't a challenging deduction by any means. Maud and I are quite well-acquainted although we are not what you would call close friends. She is a few years younger than I, although we do have some things in common. I'd waved my free arm—the one that was not clutching my cane—in the vague direction of the main area of the salon, away from the reception desk and the lavatories, and called out, "Hello Maud, how are you today?" but she mustn't have heard me because she didn't respond.

Two clients arrived shortly after I was seated, but were only in for something quick, and departed sometime before the body was discovered, whilst Alice was still slathering my hair in streaks of cold, gloopy dye.

Not long after the seat beside me was vacated, Josephine arrived, and was seated at that station, next to me, and just in front of the sinks. She greeted me cheerily, as is her way, and said how was Dennis and that her family were very well, thank you, and then she sat down for about half a minute before Gordon whisked her off to the sink and asked Lily to give her a wash. Around the time Josephine came in, so too arrived a young woman whose name I'd immediately forgotten. Clarabel? Annabel? Something with a bell, anyway.

You'd think that would have meant one of the staff was attending to each of the clients, but Flora mostly just sits at the desk and files her nails. She isn't a hairdresser by any means. The rasping can be quite irritating, after a while, but then she'll stop and flick pages of a magazine. She doesn't actually read them, because the pages turn too fast. My seat is the nearest

21

one to the desk, so I hear Flora flipping through the pages quite well. I suspect she looks at the hair styles when she is not engaged in telephone conversations. I hear those too, if the driers and chatter are not filling the air with noise. They like to seat me here, to avoid my having to navigate the rest of the room, with trolleys full of implements left in any random spot, depending on who needs dyes and who needs extensions and who needs whojamaflips or whatnots. I'd never remember where anything was parked, as they move around all over the place, and after the last time they tried to seat me further around ... well, as I say, they like me to sit in the seat nearest the door, when I come in.

Flora won't last long, I'd often thought. *I'd put my pension on it*. She always seemed terribly aloof and didn't seem at all interested.

Aside from washing Josephine's hair, Lily was mostly just sweeping the floor and making teas before the discovery in the cleaning cupboard. Every now and then Alice or Claude or Bobby-Jo or Gordon would call to her and ask her to fetch something, and she'd reply in a chipper voice, "I'll just pop this brush down, just a sec," or "I'll just give Mrs Whoever her cuppa, won't be a min," before rushing to do whatever she'd been bid. A scurrying little mouse, she reminds me of.

After the discovery, she did even less, but she is only a young thing, so it was understandable. They don't have the experience, do they? Of death, that is. One hopes.

So that covers the staff. Claude doesn't refer to them as his staff. "My team," he might say, or "the crew". I suppose that's young people's talk, although Claude is fifty-something if he's a day. He calls the clients "My ladies" most of the time, although that's another term that seems to be falling out of fashion, I'm afraid.

Phyllis is a dear, dear friend, and although she is a few months older than I, she can still see perfectly well, and although she will tell you her hearing is going to the dogs, it's completely untrue and I think she only says it so she can get away with eavesdropping. It had been our intention to take afternoon tea in that nice hotel on the high street, once we were 'done' in the salon, sporting our new festive hair-dos and flirting with the dashing young waiter.

I had, by sometime close to four o'clock, become resigned to postponing that little outing until such an afternoon when we were not detained in a hair salon with a corpse festering just yards away. Nonetheless, I was itching to be allowed to sit beside Phyllis and compare notes. With her eyes and my ears, we may have been able to ascertain a little more of what had occurred, during what we had expected to be a perfectly pleasant and uneventful afternoon at Claude's.

Thus, as I said, now somewhat bored with all this unproductive sitting, and at risk of becoming as stiff as the unfortunate corpse if I stayed immobile for very much longer, I feigned an urgent need to visit the lavatory, and tapped my way across the room. I was good at finding things out, you see. People are unsuspecting of a nearly-blind old woman.

Phyllis spotted me even though she was behind the dividing mirror—as I said, she is blessed with quite exceptional eyesight for someone of seventy-five—and I attempted a little detour in the direction of her voice only to be accosted by an arm.

"Do you need some help?" The voice belonging to the female police officer was soft but firm, allowing no room for argument. She told me she was a detective sergeant, which didn't surprise me at all as she gave off quite the air of competency as she steered me gently away from Phyllis. I supposed she must have a very serious face and wondered if she had her hair tied back in one of those neat chignon styles, or perhaps she liked to keep it cropped short, for convenience. She'd have made an excellent teacher.

"I need to visit the ladies' room," I told her. "Am I going the wrong way? All this noise and hubbub is upsetting my sense of direction." It was a little white lie, but one never knows when it may be useful to appear helpless.

She patted my arm in the matter of one comforting the dying. "Let me help you."

If there is one thing I have learned, it's that people are more inclined to share information with a batty-but-harmless old woman than with a sharp-witted ex-teacher, especially when they believe she can't see a thing. Not that any of the lights and shadows I can make out are of any great use in that department.

I allowed the police officer to guide me to the lavatory, taking full advantage of her presence to quiz her on the situation. "What is going on? It's most disconcerting. My Dennis will be wondering where I've got to and he won't know what to have for his dinner. Do you think we will be here very much longer?"

She spoke in phrases designed to be comforting without patronising and I found myself wondering whether there might be a textbook of stock platitudes taught at police training college for these kind of situations. She accompanied me all the way into the lobby of the ladies' room and I sensed her hesitation as she weighed up the extent of my capabilities.

"Do you—"

"I can manage myself perfectly well, thank you, dear. You go on back to your investigating and I will be perfectly fine in here alone." I reached out vaguely in the direction of her voice and patted the air, dismissing her.

"If you are sure ..." She wasn't convinced, but I could tell she had no desire to help an old woman down with her knickers either.

I laughed, because really, what else can one do when a stranger is unsure whether you can be trusted not to piddle on the floor or fall into the handbasin? "Really, dear, I can manage perfectly. But if it reassures you, you may wait outside the door and whistle. You can tell me what's going on out there in the broom cupboard while you wait."

The air shifted and rustled, and I imagined her to have leaned back against the wall and eased the weight from one of her feet. The queen used to do that, you know? A little knack she had for those long periods of tedious standing around smiling at people and being gracious while all the time I expect her bunions ached and her toes throbbed.

I tapped my way into the lavatory cubicle and closed the door, felt for the loo-roll holder and rested my cane against it before fumbling with my tights and undergarments. "Tell me, dear," I called through the closed door, "has the unfortunate man been identified?"

"How do you know it's a man?" Her voice teetered on the edge of curious and suspicious.

I wanted to tell her that only a man could smell that bad, but restrained myself on two counts of sensibility: one, this wasn't the place for a joke, and two, I was quite content to keep my aces up my sleeve at this point. I would not let her know that my sense of smell is as acute as that of a hungry fox; not yet.

"Oh, the young lady attending to my hair said so. She saw him first."

"But you found him, I believe?"

"I didn't know it was a body. I presumed it to be a pile of soiled laundry. It was quite pliable, you see."

I realise that I am telling this in something of a muddle. It is increasingly difficult to keep things straight, at seventy-four. You'll understand when you get there, I'm sure. My mind is a sharp as a flu-vaccination when it pierces my ever-thinning skin, but I do get in a muddle with maintaining the order of things. I have, of course, already told you the name of the corpse, but it was only as we conversed, one each side of the lavatory door, and I with my undergarments around my ankles, that Detective Sergeant Sana Nasir presented me with that information. And her name, before you ask. His name first, then her own. I immediately reimagined her in my mind, wondering if she was wearing one of those headscarves—a hijab or a whojamaflip. An old woman can get away with a little bluntness, and with the door firmly closed between us, I took the liberty of asking her, and then we had the most interesting conversation about a new style of hijab designed especially for Muslim police officers in 2019 and it was most fascinating and I almost forgot about the poor dead man in the cleaning cupboard.

I tidied myself up, flushed, and patted the door until I found the lock. As I rinsed my hands, I returned the topic to the corpse. "Robert J. Robertson, hmm?"

"Did you know him?"

I hadn't, not exactly, although I did think I may have heard his name at some point or other, because you'll agree it's a name you might remember once you've heard it about town once or twice, but I don't believe I'd ever met the man or had anything to do with him. He can't have gone to school here in Little Wittering, at least, not in my time. I still sit on the Board of Governors, so I do keep abreast of things. Of course, I no longer know every pupil who passes through Little Wittering Primary or St Cuthbert's Secondary, but if he were an outstanding student, his name would have come up; they usually do. Students who achieve well, and students who do not. Outstanding at both ends of the scale. We don't tend to discuss the mediocre, head-down-and-get-on-with-it types. Robert J. Robertson would have almost certainly been in the second category of Outstanding if he is the kind of man to find himself dead in a broom cupboard, you can be quite sure.

"A troublemaker, was he?" I asked D.S. Nasir as she placed a paper towel into my hand.

"Why do you say that?"

Don't think I hadn't noticed that she answered my questions with questions of her own. It's another little trick I expect they teach in police training college. Teachers use it too, but usually only for those outstanding troublemakers I was telling you about.

I said as much to the detective—about the troublemakers, that is—and I could tell she agreed with me, although she did say in quite a firm voice that she couldn't possibly divulge whether Robert J. Robertson was a troublemaker, as they didn't yet know very much about him. Which was fair enough, as they had only been in the salon for about thirty minutes, and so far most of that appeared to have been used up in guarding the doors so we couldn't escape and wondering in *sotto voce* about how much longer the doctor would be.

Chapter Three

As it happened, the first thing D.S. Nasir said as she guided me back into the salon was, "Oh, there he is!" to which I said, "Who?" and she replied, "The doctor."

She said, "One minute," in a voice projected in such a direction I knew she wasn't speaking to me, and led me to my seat, which was unfortunate as it took away any further chance of my speaking with Phyllis, or anyone else for that matter, and then the lovely Detective Sergeant strode away in those sensible shoes to greet the doctor.

It wasn't entirely necessary for her to go to him, if you ask me, as Doofus Finbury and the other policeman were already dealing with the doctor's arrival. Had it been Finbury alone, you would see the point, but the other one came across as eminently capable. It wasn't, you will be pleased to note, Dr Hornsby. He may be refusing to retire, but he is most certainly *not* the doctor one would call out to any level of emergency.

I strained to catch the voice, but as Finbury's high-pitched babble cut through every other noise including the pneumatic drill at work further along the high street in front of the Co-op, I couldn't tell whether it was Dr Foote or Dr Patil who had arrived on the scene. It had to be one or the other, because

D.S. Nasir had said "he", and I do notice details. Both these men were perfectly pleasant and quite good at their jobs, but if pushed, I would have to express a slight preference for Dr Patil. His hands are a little warmer, as is his bedside manner, although he does speak rather fast. Dennis would choose Dr Foote, so you see we are still quite independent in our thoughts despite having been married for fifty-two years.

I settled back into the squeaky faux-leather salon chair and swivelled it around a little with my foot until I was facing the desk, where the police officers and the doctor seemed to be conferring, as far as I could tell. Before I could catch any of the conversation, Alice returned, bearing yet another cup of tea. I imagined an ongoing loop of tea and trips to the lavatory for the rest of my time on this earth, trapped here in a salon and wondering, as the hours ticked on, if perhaps I had passed away and this was, in fact, the waiting room to the afterlife; some kind of Purgatory.

Alice, despite still being all of a fluster, set the tea into my hands with barely any slopping this time around. "I brought you more tea, Mrs Smith," she said, with a breathless shudder.

"Yes dear. I guessed it wasn't gin, from the warmth of the cup."

"Gin would be good right now." She sighed and sniffed again.

"Alice, dear, do go and fetch a chair from somewhere and sit down here beside me. I am quite sure there is nothing else you can do right now, and you *have* had a nasty shock. I am certain that lovely policewoman will quite understand, and she outranks that imbecile Finbury, so you don't need to worry about him." I don't call him Doofus aloud, of course. Except to Dennis. We don't have secrets from one another, not at our age. And to Phyllis. Phyllis and I share everything. Did I mention we have been friends for longer even than I have known Dennis? We met in teaching college, when we were seventeen, and that is far longer ago than I wish to recall.

I did so wish I could go and sit with Phyllis.

Alice did as I'd suggested, and with a scrape and a clunk and a soft whoosh of air, she sat beside me. It must have been an empty hair-styling chair she had dragged over, judging by the weight of it scraping over the floor. In between sniffs, she slurped and swallowed in little hissy noises as if her drink was too hot but she had nothing better to do than drink it anyway. She had my full sympathy, as the day had become more than a little tedious by that point. I was sure *some* people were reading their books or magazines quite happily, but I wouldn't have listened to my audiobook even if our telephones and such other electronic devices had not been confiscated by then, in case it prevented me from hearing anything exciting.

The best course of action, therefore, was to put our heads together and see if we could get to the bottom of things and speed all this along so we could all get off home.

"Now then," I said, in the low voice I used to use in St Cuthbert's, when I needed a pupil to confide in me. You might call it telling tales, but we teachers called it *You'd better tell me everything. You won't get into any trouble if you tell the truth, there's a good lad.* Or girl. It was *usually* the boys, of course. "You can be my eyes. Tell me what is going on. Who did you find in the cupboard and what, exactly was he doing there?"

I didn't let on that D.S. Nasir had already told me the poor man's name, in case Alice had anything more useful to add.

I was unprepared, however, for her to burst into fresh and noisy sobs. She set her mug onto the shelf with a clatter of heavy earthenware meeting glass and I worried that she may have cracked something, but she didn't say so, so it was probably the durable kind of glass. One supposes it must be, in a salon.

"Whatever is the matter?"

In between snotty sniffles and the ruffling of paper tissues, she told me something quite surprising. I am sure if she had not been snuffling into those tissues, she would have noticed my mouth hung open for just long enough for me to hear my grandmother's voice echoing in my head: "Do close your mouth, Sally Amanda. Do you wish to swallow flies?" Of course, I barely remember my grandmother, but there are always one or two lingering memories of loved ones, however long ago they passed from this world.

Alice, as it turned out, had known the dead man quite intimately. I hope you won't be too shocked to hear they had been *lovers*. People nowadays do all manner of things without committing to marriage, but it wasn't like that when Dennis and I married. I am certainly not a prude, and I imagine it can be immensely useful to ensure one is compatible before going through all that palaver of a wedding ceremony, especially given the astronomical expense of weddings, these days. My granddaughter is soon to be married, but I can't tell you how much she is planning to spend because my daughter tells me the shock of it would kill me and she doesn't want to be responsible for that. So, overall, it is a very useful modern concept to test-drive the goods, as it were. After all, one is permitted to test a swatch of wallpaper or return a faulty kettle, so why not a man? I am most fortunate that my Dennis, despite the odd inevitable shortcoming, would never be considered *faulty*. I will admit, I *have* tried for fifty years to persuade the man not to ball his socks before placing them in the laundry, and it is far too late to hope he will one day manage to cook a full roast dinner for us, but he has always been very handy at DIY, and he maintained our garden beautifully until his gout got in the way. One can't complain.

Alice sniffed again.

"Have a good blow, for goodness sake, and then tell me all about it."

She blew noisily, took a deep, juddering breath, and blew again. After a few moments of that, the scrape of the mug on the glass told me she had composed herself enough to regather her faculties. I had expected her to have tea, given the circumstances, but the wafting aroma of coffee swirled into my nostrils as she lifted the cup. I was glad of that, to be perfectly honest, as the long hours spent in this steamy environment were inducing sleepiness, and with little to do to occupy myself, I feared I may be in some danger of nodding off.

I inhaled the caffeine-rich brew and straightened myself in the seat. "Now, Alice, tell me *exactly* what you know about him. We may as well try to work out what has happened while we are confined, don't you think?"

"It ended a few weeks ago. We aren't together *now*."

That much seemed obvious. Robert J. Robertson was quite clearly not *together* with anyone except his maker at that precise moment, but I didn't want to set her off again, so I nodded and made encouraging noises.

She'd been seeing him—such a funny turn of phrase, don't you think?—for about six months, she said, with the odd quavery sniffle, but they had parted ways in November. A suspiciously recent split, I thought, considering he was now dead in the broom cupboard, but I didn't voice this observation, and of course it could simply be an unlucky coincidence.

"Were you very disappointed?"

"Oh goodness, Mrs Smith, no! The man was an idiot!"

"But you were together for six months? Was he *always* an idiot or was that a new development?"

She giggled at that, so I got the impression she wasn't heartbroken over their parting, although it was quite a feeble sound. Better than the crying, nonetheless.

"He was always an idiot. I just didn't realise it at first."

"What made you realise?"

"He was quite a—" She broke off abruptly, although I'm sure whichever uncouth word had been on the tip of her tongue would have been nothing I hadn't heard before. "—quite *unpleasant*, once I got to know him better."

Aha! As I predicted. The man was a troublemaker. One can always recognise the type, if one has been a teacher for over forty years.

"In what way was he unpleasant? Did he ball his socks before placing them in the laundry? My Dennis is a terror for it, but he redeems himself in other ways."

She giggled again at that, although it was still a terribly feeble sound, much like one hears from a new lamb bleating for its mother. She nudged my arms with hers, causing me to gasp and clasp my hand to my mouth and slop a little more of my tea onto my leg.

"Alice! Goodness gracious! You young people have the minds of sewer rats." I am far beyond the age of blushing, and in any case, just between you and me, she did have a valid point. Dennis had always been ... well ... "He is useful with his tools," I added quickly, but that seemed to cause a fresh wave of giggles, so I gave up and let her giggle it out.

It was quite some moments before she composed herself, after which she continued to tell me about the deceased man in the cupboard. "It was such a shock, Mrs Smith, to see him lying there, with his head bashed in. I recognised him at once."

Well, I thought to myself, now we are getting somewhere. That explains the smell of blood. What excitement! I sat up even straighter in my chair and leaned towards her, conspiratorially. "His head bashed in? Goodness! With what?"

She had no idea about that, having merely taken in the sight of her dead ex-lover; screamed, and backed from the room into the waiting arms of those who had rushed to investigate the upset.

I suppose it was understandable.

"Well," I asked, as if I were interrogating a child who had mislaid some homework. "What implements are located in that cupboard that might be hefty enough to bash someone on the head hard enough to kill him? I presume there are no candlesticks or lengths of lead piping, so what else could be utilised as a murder weapon?"

One tends to not use lead, these days, of course; not for piping or paint or even toy soldiers, so that would be most unlikely, but Alice didn't seem to get the reference because she said, "Why on earth would there be a candlestick in the broom cupboard?" in a high-pitched, raised-eyebrows kind of voice.

After that, she remained silent for a long moment, in which we both considered the possibilities. Well, that is to say, I considered the possibilities and I assume she did too, because the next thing she said was that they did have some of those scented air-freshener things with wicks and perfume that come in a heavy glass jar, and would that be a thing one might be able to bash someone over the head with?

"Yes," I said. "I imagine it might do very well."

In truth, I didn't think one of those *was* the murder weapon, because if something so strongly perfumed as a vanilla air freshener *had* been used to crack Robert J. Robertson about the head, you would imagine it would have left a lingering scent of the perfume in its wake, and there was most certainly not a smell of anything *pleasant* in that cupboard. I didn't say any of this to Alice, as I didn't want to discourage her, so I nodded, to show I was taking her seriously, and said, "Can you think of anything else?"

"Big bottles of shampoo? They weigh an absolute ton. Conditioner, too."

I asked if they were that soft kind of plastic that dents when you prod at it, or the firm, stiffer kind, and she said she supposed they were somewhere in between, and it would probably give someone an awful headache if you bashed them with one, but maybe wouldn't be enough to kill them and you'd have to be awfully strong to lift it, anyway.

I sensed she was beginning to give this quite some thought, but I have to say I agreed with her analysis and didn't imagine a shampoo bottle would be an entirely successful murder weapon, somehow, especially as it sounded as if it would be quite awkward to lift one high enough to hit someone on the head.

"What kind of things are kept in that cupboard? Let's not worry about suitability as a murder weapon, but merely list the items stored? It might give us some inspiration."

For the next few minutes we amused ourselves with our own little adaptation of the My Aunt Went to Paris game, in which Alice recited, "In Claude's Cleaning Cupboard, Claude keeps ..." In this fashion, she reeled off a long list including towels, both clean and dirty, and various cleaning supplies from brushes and dustpans to bottles of bleach to a mop and bucket to a vacuum cleaner. This last, she informed me, in case it mattered, was one of those cute Henry ones with a cheerful face, except, she added, not actually a Henry but a George. George, apparently, is the Henry that can shampoo carpets, which seems unnecessary, if you ask me, as there are no carpets in Claude's Curls.

"Oh, no, we use him to wash the floor," she said, with another giggle.

I was glad that this silly little game was cheering her up. Recanting the usual contents of the cupboard seemed to be keeping her mind off the day's more unusual content of the cupboard: the dead man. Nonetheless, the thought of him was never far from our minds, given the bustling of the police officers and the arrival of two paramedics and an ambulance, ready to remove the corpse as soon as permission was granted.

It seemed somewhat ironic that the only person in the salon who had nowhere to go anymore would be the first one permitted to leave, but I kept that thought to myself in case it was in poor taste, and was immediately proved wrong by the departure of the doctor, who said in a serious, bedside-manner kind of voice that the man was very much dead and could be removed to the mortuary as soon as the police gave the go-ahead, and then I didn't hear him again, so I presume that was when he left.

The salon felt very busy by this time, with the paramedics chatting jovially in matter-of-fact, normal-voices, and all the hairstylists except Claude flittering about between clients, trying to keep on top of things, while Claude was somewhere over by the desk talking to the officials.

All this must have made the area around Flora's reception desk and the front of the salon quite crowded, and the shadows blurred and shifted but I couldn't make any kind of guess as to what any of them actually looked like. Snippets of disjointed conversation drifted through the salon, but they mostly talked about football and whether it might snow before Christmas.

The policeman who wasn't Finbury said something about not moving the body just yet, and he'd be as quick as he could, but you know how these things are, so I suppose the officers still had to do whatever it was they needed to do to gather evidence.

One of the paramedics replied in a booming voice that made me think he probably had a beard that they'd just wait here and chat to the receptionist, to which Claude replied, "She'll get you a nice cup of tea while you wait," which they agreed to quite easily.

I suspected Claude wanted to send Flora off out of the way so she couldn't chatter unprofessionally about the dead man, and she clip-clopped past the lavatories and the cupboard, and away to the staff room; her steps faltering just a little at probably around about the spot where she had to pass the cleaning cupboard. By then, the light filtering through the large front window was significantly dimmer than when I had first arrived at the salon, so either the crowd of people was blocking the last remnants of daylight, or it was already fully dark outside.

"What *is* the time, Alice?"

"Ten past four. We'll be closing soon." She must have said that automatically, without thinking through the sense of her words, as the salon had been closed ever since Dougal Finbury's arrival, and I had heard Flora unlocking and relocking the door on four separate occasions aside from letting in the police officers or the paramedics, to explain, "No, sorry, you can't come in, there's been an incident," or, "You could pop down the road to the other salon but I doubt they've room, this close to Christmas."

Three of the four she turned away were most displeased about their cancelled appointments. Two of those became quite argumentative, and shouted at her a bit, which was unfair, as it wasn't Flora's fault. At least, I hoped it wasn't, but it had to be *somebody's* and in truth, Flora, like the rest of us, *was* a suspect, as far as I could tell.

On those occasions, Dougal Finbury showed himself to be not entirely without use, as he clumped to the door and growled at them to go away; there was a police matter to deal with and no one had time to argue and could Flora please close the door immediately to keep the temperature ambient. I was surprised he knew such a word, as in school his spelling was bottom of the class and his written work was on the level of an illiterate monkey given a pencil to play with. He pronounced it as *om-by-ont* which proves that some things never change, however much one is taught in police training college. Nonetheless, it did the trick, and the door was closed and the ambience restored. I do hope dear Claude doesn't lose clients over this unfortunate situation, the poor man.

"Alice," I said, once she had exhausted the list of supplies and paraphernalia stored in the cupboard and could think of nothing else, "we also have some other crucial pieces of information to consider."

"What're they, then?"

"Firstly," I said, holding up a finger as if I were teaching a class of four-year-olds, "we must consider *who* could have taken it upon themselves to bash a man over the head in the cleaning cupboard."

Alice gasped. She is not the kind of person to wear pearls, but had she been that kind of person, I have no doubt she would have been clutching at them in shock. Her gasp was a mix of surprise, shock, horror, and disbelief. When one can no longer read people's faces, one learns to interpret the sounds they make, even when they do not speak. Had the poor dear girl not realised that in order to have one's head bashed in, someone else, inevitably, must have done the bashing?

I spoke in a low whisper into Alice's shocked silence. "And to discover that, we must deduce two very important factors."

"Um ..." Alice, it seemed, had become inarticulate, so I expanded on my theory.

"We must discover exactly *when* the murder was committed, and we must discover *why* the murder was committed."

Chapter Four

"Could it not have been an accident?" Alice asked, with an edge of desperate hope in her voice that I imagined echoed everyone's sentiments about the matter.

"It most certainly could," I agreed, "but one would suppose if it had been an accident, the poor man would not have been left there, unattended, but that the perpetrator might have called for help."

"Hmm, suppose," she said, and slurped noisily at her coffee.

"Tell me more about Robert J. Robertson," I suggested. "Let's see what we can determine."

The dead man's crime, it transpired, was a far greater misdemeanour than balling his socks, and far less forgivable.

"He was a horrible man and he was cheating on me," she whispered, with a tremor in her voice, as if somehow it reflected badly on her own character.

I'm not one to jump to conclusions, so I remained open-minded about that, and said, "Oh my," in what I hoped was a sympathetic tone. "That must have been a terrible shock." I said no more, for danger of influencing the direction of her next words. In my many decades in the classroom, I learned the benefits of holding one's silence during a fact-finding mission. It is human nature to fill a gap in a conversation, and as such, silence is a tactic I believe to be long-employed by the police as well as by teachers.

Sure enough, Alice obliged. "With Flora." Her whisper was laced with venom, and I deduced immediately that there was no love lost between the two colleagues. "He cheated on me with *Flora*."

"Flora the receptionist?" I balanced my tone with a careful mix of sympathy and incredulity, and turned my head towards the reception desk, even though I hadn't yet heard the irksome woman clip-clop back from the staffroom with the paramedics' tea.

"Yes." It came out as a low hiss, and I suspected Alice was also glaring in the direction of the reception desk or towards whichever corner of the room her enemy may be skulking within.

"I'm terribly sorry," I said, truthfully. I imagine it is never pleasant to discover one is the victim of infidelity, but to work alongside the new object of your lover's affections must be a bitter pill indeed. "You realised you disliked him, then, after that?" I added, conversationally, keeping my voice level and unaccusing.

"You could say that." Alice gave a low, bitter chuckle, devoid of humour. "Almost as much as I dislike *her*." Although we were keeping our voices low so as not to draw the attention of Doofus or his colleagues, Alice still managed to spit the words into the air with dagger-sharp enunciation and I recoiled slightly in my chair.

"Goodness, Alice, you sound quite dangerous. You must have wanted to kill them both." Again, I maintained a calm, even tone, and she immediately fell into the trap.

"Yes I bloody did! Oops, sorry, Mrs Smith, excuse my French!"

French! It had been a while since I'd heard that expression, I can tell you. Not since my teaching days, I shouldn't wonder. Language notwithstanding, I waited a beat before replying, wondering if the penny would drop, and of course it did.

There was an abrupt gasp of air and the soft slap of a hand against lips. "Oh! I ... I didn't mean ... I mean ... Wanting to kill someone doesn't mean I did! I didn't actually kill him, Mrs Smith! I didn't!" Her voice rose a little as she realised what she had said, and I worried Doofus would swagger across the salon and reprimand us for discussing the case.

I patted the air in front of me, feebly searching for Alice's hand. I found her arm, and rested my fingers lightly on her sleeve. "Shh, shh. Of course you didn't. It's just a figure of speech. Hush now."

Somewhere within the room, Dougal Finbury's voice pierced the chatter.

Alice and I fell silent in order to listen.

It soon became apparent that the poor lifeless body of Robert J. Robertson was about to be transferred, and Doofus, self-important little flibbert that he is, was attempting to direct the paramedics. In my experience, paramedics rarely need direction and are inherently more capable at organising things, especially things such as handling the injured or the dead, than police officers, and I can assure you I have witnessed a good few such removals in my days.

"Careful now!" he squealed. "Mind the blood!"

"Excuse us please, Officer," retorted the no-nonsense voice of one of the paramedics—the one I imagined to be bearded. "If you could just step out of the doorway and let us get to the patient."

I was grateful they didn't refer to the poor man as a "body", or a "corpse", or even "the deceased", even though everyone in the salon knew that was exactly what he had become. It allowed the man a little dignity as the two paramedics attempted to manoeuvre him from the confines of the cupboard. I cannot imagine it was an easy job—to remove him from such a tight space—and I confess my imagination ran a little riot as I envisaged them dragging him by his feet until they could arrange him on the stretcher.

The subtle squeak of the stretcher wheels on the salon floor plotted the movements with more accuracy than Finbury, and the paramedics shifted the contraption up and down outside the cupboard for several minutes before the bearded one declared, "It's no good at all, we'll never get it in. We'll have to carry him out. Excuse me, Officer, but would you kindly stand back and give us some space?"

The second paramedic then turned *his* attention to Finbury, too, and dispatched some directions of his own: "Officer, perhaps you would be so good as to distract the onlookers?"

With a loud tut and an equally audible huff, the silly little man retorted, "There is nowhere they can go. We need to keep them here for questioning. You will just have to throw a sheet over it."

I do believe those words are a full and accurate representation of the character of the idiot child. I simply cannot fathom that any other person, in any decency, would refer to one so lately deceased as 'it', especially in full earshot of a roomful of gawping witnesses.

There were some thuds and scrapes and a few muttered instructions such as, "You take his legs; that's it now, up we go," and another squeak of the wheels and another soft thunk. A murmur of piqued interest ran around the salon, comprised of gasps and sighs and whispered platitudes. I distinctly picked out Phyllis's soft brogue as she said, "God bless him," and I have known her long enough that I can tell you with certainty that she crossed herself as the man was wheeled from the vicinity of the cupboard, and towards the street and the waiting ambulance.

Claude, although he sounded quite shellshocked by the whole affair, was pragmatic as he led the way to the door, his path across the salon tracked by his voice: "Little step here. Lily, move that plant out of the way. Bit of a squeeze here. Flora, the door, please. There we are now." I caught the tremor as he spoke, but he was, as they say, holding it together most professionally. The key clicked in the door, once, twice, to disengage the lock, followed by a sharp gust of icy air and a whoosh of high-street noise. The trolley squeak-squeaked over the threshold, accompanied by the low voices of the paramedics, the thud of footsteps, and finally, Claude's voice once more: "Well. Thank you. That's that then."

The cold draught was cut off as the door closed and the key click-clicked, and we were all locked back inside the salon again, with the exception of the paramedics and the poor dead body of Robert J. Robertson.

"Goodness," said Alice, and I agreed wholeheartedly.

After some minutes of silence, in which no one in the room spoke a word, the salon eased back into subdued chatter, most of it emanating from the police officers. The senior male policeman who'd accompanied D.S. Nasir decided he would pop out and ask a few questions of the neighbouring shops' staff, and the rigmarole of the unlocking-locking of the door was repeated as he departed into the cold night.

"Well." Finbury's petulant tones filled the room. "We'd better start talking to these customers, like? One of them must know something."

"We'll finish talking to the staff, first, establish a basic timeframe, eh?" The calm voice of D.S. Nasir put him straight, and I wondered how many times a day she found it necessary to do so.

"Ooh," whispered Alice, "they are coming this way."

The clomp of the Detective Sergeant's sensible shoes, and the irritating creak of Finbury's, coupled with the heavy breathing of an unfit constable who smokes too many Marlboros, approached the main area of the salon, and the chatter fell silent once more.

"I am sorry for the need to detain you all—" D.S. Nasir spoke confidently into the room, an air of sympathy supporting her words. "—but we do need to ask you all some questions. Take your statements; see what you saw or heard. Could I have everyone's attention for a few moments, and then once we have established some basics, we will need to interview you individually in the staffroom. It will take a while, I'm afraid."

I gathered from the direction of her voice that she had come to a halt at the head of the room, in front of the large window, and stood facing the styling chairs. I twisted my chair towards her voice, searching for a human-shaped shadow, and hoped I was turned accurately towards the detective and not merely facing a large pot plant or Christmas tree.

She asked some questions about whether any of us had anywhere pressing we needed to be, and said if anyone needed to make arrangements, we could have our telephones back for just long enough to make the necessary calls. "But other than that, I'm sorry to say, we will continue to keep your phones safely over here." I expect she meant the reception counter. She could have been gesturing to her handbag or the hair-washing basins for all I knew, but one *must* trust in an element of common sense, when one cannot rely on one's eyesight. "Just to ensure no one posts to social media, or suchlike," she added apologetically. "I must also ask you not to gossip or speculate amongst yourselves. I'm sure you understand."

A low buzz of assent rippled around the salon.

"Can we talk?" someone asked, and as I didn't recognise the voice, I imagine it must have been Annabel or Arabelle or whatever her name was.

"Keep it to the minimum?" the D.S. said. "Nothing about what's happened, okay?"

"What exactly *has* happened?" God bless Phyllis. I was quite certain she was fully aware of the situation, but I was terribly grateful to her for asking. I had every confidence she was doing her best to ensure I hadn't missed anything.

Finbury huffed self-importantly, and I could picture him puffing himself up like an amorous cockerel, swelling his chest and standing tall. "There has been a most heinous crime," he said, plucking another phrase from the policeman's handbook or a Sunday evening television detective drama. "A man has been brutally murdered."

Even though we knew this already, his over-dramatised glee and emphasis on the word "brutally" triggered a collective gasp, and the salon positively vibrated with the distinct undertone of voyeuristic excitement.

"Can we finish everyone's hair?" Gordon asked from behind me, where he had been tending to Josephine. "Only, we can't really leave people like ... like *this*."

I expect he had waved his hand around the room, wearing an expression on his face to perfectly match the horror he interjected into the word "this", and I imagined us clients huddled under aprons and towels in various stages of hairdressing, be it washing, curling, or dyeing. I shuddered at the thought of dyeing, given the circumstances, even though I have taught countless students about homophones in my time and emphasised the difference of meaning on numerous occasions, but then the very idea that we would be left *unfinished* threatened to tug my lips into a tiny smile instead. I did manage to bite my cheeks and contain the moment of inappropriate amusement, although I'm certain anyone watching me may have noticed I quickly ducked my head towards my chest to conceal my expression.

I wondered whether D.S. Nasir had similar thoughts, as when she answered Gordon, her voice was light and cheerful as she agreed that of course, the stylists should continue to do their jobs as best as they could, as she wouldn't want any of us leaving the salon half-cut. There was quite a titter at her little joke and I think we all appreciated her efforts to add some cheer to the situation.

The moment of humour was quenched by Finbury. "The cupboard is not to be entered under any circumstances. Not by anyone," he said in a most pompous tone.

"You will need to do your best with whatever you have to hand," Claude said, and I presume he was addressing his staff and not Finbury at that moment.

"Also," added D.S. Nasir, "*no one* is to leave the premises without permission from myself or my colleagues, P.C. Finbury or Detective Inspector Nelson, when he returns." She paused to let that sink in. "Now, if there are no questions for the moment, I will have another little chat with you, Claude, to draw up a list of times and people and then we will begin our interviews. P.C. Finbury will remain in this room with the rest of you. Thank you for your cooperation."

Chapter Five

The soft murmur of D.S. Nasir's and Claude's voices conferring in the waiting area drifted into the body of the salon, and Claude suggested the D.S. could first take either Bobby-Jo or Alice, as both were almost at a point where they could leave their clients for a while. Gordon, he said, was at a crucial place in Josephine's cut, but should be finished in another ten or fifteen minutes.

"Flora, you've already talked to, but if you need her again, someone else can answer the phone if needed, and I presume your constable can worry about the door. Lily, you can take anytime." Claude paused. "Where *is* Lily?" He suddenly seemed to realise she might still be sobbing in the staffroom, and said one of them should probably go and check she was all right, come to think.

It was agreed that the Detective Sergeant would first check on Lily and then dispatch her out to Claude, to give the poor child time to collect herself, and that P.C. Finbury would call Lily's mother and ask her to come in. The solid, sensible shoes stepped purposely towards the cupboard and onwards to the staffroom, and just a few minutes later, someone rapped heavily on the door of the salon and I thought Lily's mother must be either terribly efficient or miraculously nearby.

There was a rhythmic click-clacking that sometimes accompanies Flora's movements that I attribute not only to her heels, which are more of a clip-clop anyway, but to the sound of small wooden beads clacking into each other, perhaps in her hair or in a cluster of strands around her neck, although at other times, the clickety-clack is lacking so I expect she changes her hairstyle or jewellery quite frequently, as one must do if one works in a hair salon, I suppose. Then followed two sharp clicks; a flurry of cold draught, and the clunk-click-click of the door being shut and relocked, but it turned out it was only the Detective Inspector returning from his foray out into the high street.

He muttered something I couldn't catch, and a moment later, D.S. Nasir returned from the staffroom with Lily; left her with Claude in the waiting area, and whisked Bobby-Jo off to be interrogated, although she can't have had much to say as she was out again five minutes later.

"Alice," Bobby-Jo said dramatically, as if she were awarding a prize. She swept up to us in a whiff of rose, so I suspected she must have nipped into the lavatories to touch up her lipstick before returning to her duties. "It's your turn!"

I was quite brought to mind of a class of schoolgirls taking turns to visit the school nurse to get their rubella vaccination. Of course this was a very different situation, although the potential for hysterics was comparable, it must be said.

Off Alice went, obediently tripping down to the staff room to meet her fate, or at least to help with inquiries, as they like to say on the television.

No sooner had Alice left my side than Finbury loudly booted Flora out from behind the desk, telling her he'd mind the door and oversee things from here, and Flora was given the job of baby-sitting me, the doddery old blind woman, in case I needed anything.

I have never quite taken to Flora, who can be terribly abrupt, and doesn't exactly *ooze* with personable people skills, which one would think a prerequisite for a receptionist, but seemingly not. I was going to send her away, as I am most capable of minding myself, especially when all I am permitted to do is stay in a chair and not move, but just as I was about to dismiss her, the words that came from my mouth were, "I do feel a little faint, dear, so perhaps you would be good enough to sit here and chat with me for a few minutes." Of course, I felt perfectly well, but I'd had a sudden realisation that it might prove useful to hear her take on the whole unpleasant situation, her own involvement with the dead man notwithstanding.

She sighed and swished past me, emitting a faint scent of coconuts as she sank herself heavily into the chair Alice had vacated. She sighed again, and I would have been quite certain she was scrolling through her phone if not for the fact that D.S. Nasir had confiscated our telephones again after allowing us those few moments to contact our nearest or dearest to inform them of our confinement to the salon. We would, she'd explained, be permitted to make any more *absolutely necessary* calls, but they must be made within earshot of a police officer. By that point in the proceedings, I had established that when she'd informed us they would hold our phones "just over here" to prevent anyone posting to that confounded social media, she had indeed been referring to the reception desk. I'd also deduced from the clunks and thumps that Finbury had simply dumped them in a pile on the desktop, where anyone could reach them if we were permitted to stretch our legs, but I suppose there must be some element of trust amongst captives and captors as we couldn't possibly all be criminals and most of us may indeed prove to be valuable witnesses.

Perhaps then, without her phone to keep her occupied, Flora was picking at her nails or twiddling her thumbs or itching to talk and relieve the tedium.

I decided to bite the bullet, as they say. "Alice tells me you knew the poor man."

She gave a sharp intake of breath and the chair on which she sat creaked as she shifted her weight. I wondered if her face had paled, but I have always had the impression that Flora is black, given the summery scent of coconut oil that surrounds her, and I'm sure Phyllis has told me before that Flora has masses and masses of hair which she often ties up with a scarf, and I've never been entirely sure whether people with darker skin do, in fact, go pale when receiving a shock. Of course anyone with a lot of hair might do exactly the same, and I know Phyllis ties hers up with a jaunty scarf when she fancies a change so I may be entirely wrong and it is perfectly possible that Flora is a lanky, paper-faced blonde with washed-out blue eyes but such is my lot that I can only apply artistic license and imagination to create the faces of people with whom I was not acquainted before my sight failed.

Alice, who I did know before, is indeed blonde, although I imagine her hair has darkened with age, as one's hair tends to do, and the image I have of her is a decades-old memory of her aged sixteen, usually in the midst of a gaggle of schoolgirls; giggling and jostling and preening for the spotty sixth-form boys. She is not very far from Doofus in age, now that I think of it, although I don't remember if they were in the same school year or a year or two apart.

Flora, one could presume, is not a dissimilar age, if she is responsible for pilfering Alice's man, although of course one should never just *presume* such things, and who's to say there was not a significant age difference between any of the lovers? I had imagined Flora as a good bit younger, before Alice's revelation, so who knows?

Eventually, Flora answered, once again proving my theory that holding one's silence is often enough to prompt a conversation.

"What did she say? I suppose she told you I'd stolen her man." Flora's voice had an ugly edge to it; a mix of righteous defensiveness and guilty conscience, I should think.

"Why don't you tell me about it? Your side of things, that is."

Flora was silent for a moment, although the soft clacking and subtle shifts of movement led me to guess she may have been toying with her hair, or her necklace, or whatever it was that caused the clattering, and thus deep in thought, rather than refusing to speak.

Across the room, the phone shrilled on the desk, but was snatched up almost immediately by Finbury, who barked into the receiver, "We're closed," and set down the phone with a loud clunk before Flora could even get out of her seat.

She swore under her breath, and I won't repeat her words, but I must admit, I quite agreed with the sentiments.

"I used to teach him," I offered as a way to break the ice and loosen her up a little. It worked, because she said something about him that loosely translates to "I agree with you, the man's a total idiot," but used far more colourful words, and then she added that she hadn't known I was a teacher and I told her I'd been retired ever since I'd finished with his year, and she laughed and said she didn't blame me and that was enough to have us chattering away like old friends. Or at least like two people trapped in a hair salon with a trio of police officers; a murderer, and a pool of congealing blood.

"It was a stupid thing. Eugh. A one-off. The man's a total lecher," she said in a low voice, and I guessed immediately we were back to talking about Robert J. Robertson. "He came on to me in the pub one night, and I said no a few times, but he kept at it. Bought us a few drinks, persistent, like. I don't even remember, really, only the next day when I realised how much I'd had to drink did it hit me what I'd done. He took advantage, like, but I'd had a few too many to be perfectly honest, and let him come home with me, which was really, *really* stupid. I said right then when I woke up the next mornin' I wouldn't drink ever again, and then went straight out with the girls that night to drink it off and forget about him, only of course Alice found out and blamed me. I avoided him like the plague, after that, but then he got the hint and went off with someone else and that was that."

I sensed her shrug, as if her dalliance with Robert J. Robertson was a brief and unpleasant interlude that should be forgotten. "Would you indulge an old woman and describe the man to me? Was he very good looking?"

She snorted at that and I wondered whether that meant yes he was, or goodness no, or perhaps that she'd thought he was, and then realised he really wasn't after all. I didn't have to wait long for the clarification.

"Not really. He's got that kind of bad-boy charm, I suppose, that you think is good looks once you've had a drink or two, but in the cold light of a hangover, when he's snorin' there beside you and you're all bleary-eyed and can't see straight, he was nothin' special." She paused for a moment as if recalling the moment she realised she'd brought him home by mistake, much as you might accidentally pick up someone else's gloves and realise they are not yours only when they irritate your hands with their rough scratchiness. "His face was all dribbly and he looked much older, in the mornin'. Snorin' like a drunk, and the first thing he did when he woke up was try for a grope, and I wasn't havin' that, so I jumped up, threw on some scazzy old clothes, and told him it was all a mistake and I'd like him to leave."

"And did he? Leave, that is?"

"He put up a bit of a fight, to be honest, and I was a bit worried he was gonna ... well, you know? So I got my phone and told him I really wanted him to leave, please, and made out like I was already callin' someone, and I held it like I might video him and live-stream it, like, and I guess that did the trick ..." She stopped for a moment, and I felt the tremor of her chair on the floor so I supposed she must have shivered as she thought about it. "I didn't think he would go, but then he fumbled around for his clothes, told me he was at least goin' to use the bathroom, and if I hadn't been so gobsmacked by it all, I might have thought about how funny he looked, all lardy and pale and hobblin' to the bathroom with his jeans clutched to his flabby belly, but mostly I couldn't believe what I'd done. Mortified, I was, to be honest with you." She broke off again, and I imagined the scene as she'd described it and was glad that he'd left her when she'd insisted, and not tried anything else as men sometimes do if one is to believe the daily news reports.

It didn't make him sound at all like the type of man Alice should have been settling for and I couldn't help but wonder if Flora had done Alice a favour, when you came to think about it.

Flora emitted that little tremoring noise people make when they shudder, and the floor vibrated again as her chair moved. She gave a tinny little laugh. "Honestly, he wasn't as bad as all that. I'm makin' him sound worse, to make me feel better." She laughed again, although it wasn't the kind of laugh one makes when one finds something funny. "He wasn't *that* bad lookin'. He was quite buff, to be perfectly honest."

"Buff?" I asked.

"Fit. You know, toned. Like he works out. He wasn't really flabby at all. And he wasn't all that pale, like. Everyone's whiter than me, so ..." This time her laugh had more humour, and I was glad to hear I'd imagined her with some accuracy.

I asked her, then, about herself, and she confirmed it all, to my great satisfaction.

"Third gen Jamiacan, mon," she said, with an over-exaggerated accent and a proper giggle.

I'd had a sudden urge to do that thing people always think blind people do, and ask her if I could touch her face, to get a clearer idea of what she looks like, but she was already talking again and the moment passed.

"It's weird to think he's dead, though. Ugh."

"Have you and Alice made up?" Listen to me, talking to her as if she's in the playground. Once a teacher, always a teacher, as my Dennis likes to remind me, no matter how long I've been retired.

"Ah, who knows? She's frosty, like, but we weren't close anyway. I've only been here six months, and sleepin' with her man wasn't the best way to make friends."

I wasn't sure if she meant she'd only lived in Little Wittering for six months, or only been in the salon six months, which I already knew, but it didn't seem pertinent to the matter in hand, which was the murder in our midst.

"So have they told you any more about what's going on here?" I waved my hand around to encapsulate the salon and the situation. "Have they interviewed you yet?" I knew they had, as I'd heard Finbury call her to the staffroom while the paramedics were still sitting around slurping tea and waiting for backup, but I wasn't going to tell her that.

"Yeah, that thicko one took me off to the staffroom and asked me about did I know him and where was I when he was killed an' all that, and I said how would I know where I was when he was killed if I didn't know when he was killed. Then he asked if I'd gone in the cupboard and what time I got here this mornin', and had I been here when the delivery arrived. He scribbled in his little notepad and I wondered why he didn't use a phone to take notes like I thought they did these days." She snorted again. "But then I leaned in to see if he'd got my surname right, because no one ever does, and he'd just been doodlin' these little pictures all over the page and written nearly nothin'. The woman one came in then. She's all right, her. She told him she'd take it from there, and off he went like a kicked puppy."

"Did they tell you when he'd been killed?"

"No. They just said they were narrowin' it down quite nicely."

"*Had* you been in the cupboard?"

"I'm the frickin' receptionist! I never go in the cupboard, do I?"

"You don't hang your coat in there?"

"Nah, I keep mine at the desk. There's a coat stand, for the clients' coats. I put mine there too. Handy, like."

"And you don't go in for cleaning supplies, or suchlike?"

"Nah. Don't do the cleanin', do I? An' I've no need to get supplies, when I don't do the hair."

I had to think for a minute about what the other questions were that she'd said Doofus had asked her, but it came to me soon enough. "And *were* you here, when the delivery arrived?"

"Nope." Her answer was immediate and definite and in my opinion, given far too quickly to ring true.

"What was the delivery? And was it expected today? Do you usually know when a delivery is coming, that is?"

"Yeah, if it's a big delivery from the suppliers, like, then we'd have a fair idea. Time's a bit random, but the day is usually right, 'less they run out of time and show up the next day. Happens now and then, but it's usually when they say. He'd phone ahead, usually, only not since our ... our ... you know? He didn't phone ahead last time, nor this time, probably 'coz of not wanting to talk to me, I'd say."

"So you knew he was due today but not what time?"

"Right."

"Did everyone know he'd be coming today?"

"Dunno. They might've. It'd be on the calendar, like, and anyone who'd ordered anythin' would've been waitin' for it to come, and they'd have had a better idea of what was comin' when, too. Like if Gord had ordered a certain colour, for instance, he'd be watchin' for that to come, or if Claude had been waitin' on new shampoos, or whatever, but if it was just general stock that we always have, no one would bother so much."

"What time do you reckon he came, then?"

"That's the weird part, innit? No one seems to know he'd been in. He must've come at lunchtime, or before we opened, only that can't be it, 'coz the others'd be in an' out the cupboard an' someone'd have seen him sooner, like." She paused and clacked her hair some more. "Lemme see ... I got in bang on nine today. Bit late, 'coz the bus was slow, what with it being nearly Christmas, an' busy an' all that. I'm meant to get here by ten to; ready for when the first clients come in."

"Were there clients waiting, when you arrived?"

"Only two. I met them on the doorstep. Quick wash-and-blow-dry, both of them. Only here about half an hour, I'd say. The next ones didn't come in until quarter past."

"Who of the staff was here when you arrived?"

"Most of them, I think." She paused, as if sifting through her mind for the memory, and I took a moment to reflect that perhaps I'd misjudged the girl; she was perfectly pleasant once you got talking to her.

"Claude wasn't, because he always nips out first thing to get us something for the staffroom. He usually comes in about half-eight, checks some stuff, then goes out again, like.

Donuts, it was, today. Gord was here already, because he did one of the nine o'clocks, an' they usually come in together anyway, him an' Claude, of course. Bobby-Jo took the other nine o'clock, so she was in early and away early, too, for somethin' or other at her little boy's school. Alice came in a minute or two after me, I'd guess. Lily only comes in at nine-thirty because her mam drops her off after she takes her brothers to school, and there's not much for her to do before that, anyway."

This provided me with a perfect opening to gather some information about the student.

Lily, Flora explained, was the latest of an ever-changing assortment of students from the college. She wasn't the worst they'd had in Claude's Curls, in the six months since Flora had been working there, but she couldn't see Claude taking her on, not when the poor girl had no initiative. "She needs to be told what to do. All the time. She does it all right, but she does need to be *told*."

"Would the students ever get to cut anyone's hair?" I'd asked, with a shudder. I couldn't imagine someone untrained being let loose with a pair of scissors and a paying customer.

"Not at her level. The Second Years do, sometimes, if Claude's confident. They practice at college, first, like. Not Lily, though. She rocked up at nine-thirty, ish, pushed the broom around a bit, made some tea, cleaned a mirror, and shot out the door for lunch at ten to twelve. Not meant to go 'til twelve, but she said somethin' about needin' to get her mam's Christmas present, and it's not up to me."

"What did she buy? Did she say?"

"Not a clue. She strolled in a bit after one, casual as you like, not a word about being late, dumped her stuff in the staffroom, and I couldn't say what she's been at since. Before ... before, that is. Since then, she's been mostly snifflin' and cryin' and askin' if she can go home yet. But then she is only sixteen or so. Poor thing. She's all right, really."

"It must have been a terrible shock to you all." I waited a beat. "Except one, of course."

"Huh?"

"Well someone in here must have killed the poor man."

Chapter Six

The opening and closing of a door somewhere beyond the lavatories; a sudden lull in the quiet conversations around the salon, and the soft pitter-patter of approaching shoes left me unsurprised when Alice's gentle voice confirmed her return.

"You okay there, Mrs Smith? That nice detective woman asked me to check in on you and make sure you're comfortable. Said to let you know it could be a while yet."

I must admit I was surprised at the decision of the police to question the salon staff before the clients, as it seemed to me they would be able to weed most of the clients from the investigation quite easily, and could have tackled that first and let us get off home to our husbands or our tea, or whatever it was we needed to get home to. Perhaps they concluded that by keeping us confined, any gossip about the situation would be restricted to within Claude's Curls, and not let out in public, as it were. I don't know much about this new-fangled social media, but I suppose even the likes of Phyllis and me might be inclined to let something slip, just in passing conversation as we went about our day. One can't be too careful, I suppose, with a murder investigation, and I could see that it made some degree of sense for the police to establish the salon's schedule, so perhaps that was why they started with the staff. All this made me feel quite relieved I had never decided to become a police officer, as on certain days even teaching was quite enough of a challenge, and that was without contending with dead bodies or cold-blooded killings, despite what you may envisage in a school during the difficult period leading up to an Ofsted inspection.

Nonetheless, I was quite certain that Mr Robertson had not entered Claude's Curls at any time since the salon had opened for its afternoon business, and therefore his death must have occurred either during the morning or during lunchtime. If the salon had been as busy with clients throughout the morning as it was that afternoon, I simply couldn't imagine anyone could get away with murder while the salon was open for business. If I were the police officers, I would be looking very closely at the times of day before the salon opened, or while it was closed for lunch, and if Flora was correct, and the salon staff had been traipsing in and out of the cupboard all day long, then the lunchtime window was really the only logical time anyone could have murdered Robert J. Robertson, in my opinion.

Therefore, it also followed that those of us who arrived at Claude's Curls only after the salon reopened at one o'clock must be in the clear, as it were. I could personally vouch for both Phyllis and myself, as we had arrived together at exactly one o'clock that afternoon, as corroborated by the chiming of the town clock, which does keep immaculate time and has never, as long as I have known, been mistaken in its chiming. Of the afternoon's other customers, to the best of my knowledge, only Maud preceded us, as Flora had to unlock the doors to let us enter but Maud, by then, had already been admitted by Alice. So you can see that Phyllis, Josephine, and Isobel or Annabel or whatever her name was, and the handful of clients who had been and gone, and I, of course, were entirely without opportunity to have murdered anyone in the salon's cleaning cupboard, and as such, we should all have been eliminated immediately from the enquiries. No one of us, I am quite sure, would have been able to admit entry to a delivery man, bludgeon him to death, and leave him in a pool of his own blood without it being noticed, even had we become overcome by an inexplicable urge to do so.

The cupboard in which the poor man perished was not beside the front door, nor was it tucked away out of sight. (Not to those blessed with vision, that is. It goes without saying that *I* couldn't see it.) In order to reach the cupboard, the lavatories, and the staff room, one must pass the reception desk and fully enter the salon, and in order to reach the lavatories, one must pass the cupboard. The layout is as such:

Upon entry into the salon, one is greeted by a smooth curve of Flora's desk, which fills the corner to the right-hand side of the door and faces into the room, rather than onto the street as one might expect. Flora, I believe, sits with her back to the window, or perhaps sideways on, with her back to the wall. I expect she has one of those nice swivel chairs and adjusts her view to suit her mood or activity. The main door into the salon from the high street sits off-centre, perhaps midway between the centre point and the right-hand wall dividing Claude's Curls from the off-licence next door, although I cannot tell you that with certainty, only the reliance of old memory and an awareness of the space inside.

Beyond Flora's desk, as one progresses towards the back of the property, there sits a neat L-shaped bench seat upon which clients may wait. It is upholstered in squeaky wipe-clean something-or-other, and faces both towards the desk and into the main part of salon, depending upon which side of the L one chooses to sit and the capabilities of one's eyesight. I, of course, see neither, although I am aware of the angle of the window if the day is bright. In front of the bench-seating is a low table adorned with magazines and a pungent plant of some kind. I do prefer it when a business displays real plants, don't you? Those artificial replicas smell so terribly strongly of rubber and are a haven for dust. Each time I visit Claude's, he or Alice or whoever it may be who welcomes me in always reminds me to mind the table, ever since I stumbled into it on one unforgotten occasion and bruised my shin most painfully. I cannot tell you what species of plant is on the table, but on that particular Thursday it had been freshly watered, releasing that damp, earthy smell one notices after heavy rain on a freshly-dug flowerbed.

Beyond the bench seat, one comes first to the cupboard, which is used predominately for storage of cleaning materials and hairdressing supplies, but on the Thursday in question, also for bumping off and concealing the congealing corpse of Robert J. Robertson.

Beyond this, as I have said, is the ladies' lavatory, and to the best of my belief, and unless the layout has been amended within the past decade, the gentlemen's facilities are situated beyond that; the last stop before the staff room, which was, until turned over as a makeshift interview room, out of bounds to the salon's clientele. It is good practice to set the gents' lavatories to the rear, beyond the ladies', as one tends to find men's toilets to be significantly more odorous, don't you agree? I, fortunately, had never found it necessary to venture beyond the ladies' lavatories, at least not until the day of Robert J. Robertson's inconvenient demise, and to be perfectly fair, the gentlemen's facilities, being used only by Claude and Gordon, one supposes, do not smell overly offensive, as far as I have surmised.

Thus is the layout of the right-most side of the premises as one enters the salon from the high street.

The rest of the space is committed to the actual business of hairdressing: the styling chairs; the sinks, and so forth. The sinks are situated to the back of the room, set upon a plinth, two steps higher than the main floor, and distinctly awkward to negotiate when one is dripping and gowned and attempting to keep one's towels in place whilst simultaneously brandishing a cane or holding an arm. It is a most inconvenient design, and not a good planning decision by any means, particularly if one is hindered by accessibility difficulties. There are five or six stylists' chairs, or quite possibly as many as seven, not including those chairs set at the sinks for the washing of one's hair, of which I think there are only two. Four of the styling chairs are arranged in two pairs, face-to-face, in the centre of the room, divided by large mirrors and whatnots. The other styling chairs are set against the far wall, beyond where I am permitted to sit, and back-to-back with Phyllis and Maud. There is space enough between each neighbouring chair that one cannot easily confer with one's neighbour without raising one's voice and straining one's ears, especially when the salon is thrumming with noise. This situation is one

I usually find most agreeable, but on the day of the incident, I would have much preferred the ability to freely indulge in conversation with my neighbours.

When Josephine arrived, she had, at least initially, been sat in the chair next to mine, and attended to by Gordon, but I wasn't entirely certain if she had remained there throughout, as those unhindered by faulty eyesight are sometimes moved from one seat to another as their hairdressing progresses through its various stages.

Phyllis was frustratingly nearby, yet too distant for us to confer, as although we faced each other, our chairs were divided by the wall of mirrors between us. I am habitually grateful for the spacious interior of this salon—it makes it so much easier to navigate when one has sufficient open floor space—but that day I would have traded my last cup of tea to have been close enough to my dear friend that we may have compared our observations regarding the unfolding murder mystery. I so longed for us to put our freshly-coiffed heads together to see if we couldn't reach some conclusions of our own about the whole affair.

Maud, I believe, had spent the afternoon stationed in the corner diagonal to me; opposite Josephine, and next to Phyllis.

The fifth client, whose name I still hadn't managed to determine at that point, was situated somewhere against the far wall, and from the direction of her voice when she spoke, I placed her behind Phyllis—back-to-back, presumably—but closer to the window. It is perfectly plausible that I may be incorrect in some of these placings. It can be so hard to be certain when all around is the buzz of chatter; the whirr of hair-dryers, and the almost constant desire of hair stylists to probe one about one's holidays when all one wishes is to sit in the peace of one's own thoughts. Alice, it must be said, has learned my preferences in this matter. She is meticulous in keeping me informed of her actions and progress relating to my hair, but wastes no time with idle chitchat about holidays or whatnot, unless I initiate such topics. It must also be said that since the discovery of the body at approximately two-forty that afternoon, *no one* in Claude's Curls had talked about holidays, or least not that I heard.

I am well-acquainted with Josephine and we have much in common. She is currently employed as a Special Needs Assistant in the primary school, although in times past she has also worked in St Cuthbert's. She is a good decade or so younger than me and must be approaching retirement, although she certainly hasn't retired yet, so I wondered what she was doing in the hair salon in the middle of the afternoon on the last Thursday before Christmas. One would think she should have been busy with the nativity play. Perhaps whoever it is she supports was not permitted to participate in the play, although that would not be in keeping with the policies of inclusivity schools are supposed to promote these days and terribly unkind, so maybe her charges were sick or she had been granted some other reprieve. As I had yet to speak with her beyond our initial cheerful greetings when she had arrived, I couldn't draw any real conclusions about that, but when one finds time on one's hands and is able to sit and reflect on things, one does find the imagination prone to such speculative ramblings.

The other client, who I do *think* Alice had referred to as Annabel, is not someone I know at all, but as she had arrived an hour or so after Phyllis and me, it hardly seemed important. It seemed highly improbable that she could be the murderer, whatever her name may be.

In the interim between Phyllis and I arriving at one o'clock, and the discovery of the corpse some ninety minutes later, two other clients had come and gone, but as neither had been here alone at any time in the afternoon, they could hardly be considered likely suspects and I had caught no wind of any of the police officers worrying about them.

Josephine had arrived quite some time after Phyllis and me, and if I were pressed, I would estimate her time of arrival to be around one-forty-five. Bobby-Jo had returned some time before Josephine's arrival, now I think about it, so the nativity play had finished and I suppose Josephine had the afternoon off, which was nice. Josephine was in the salon a good fifteen minutes before the woman I shall refer to as Annabel whether that is or is not her actual name, for the sake of clarity. I am quite confident of this, because Josephine had time to get her hair washed, be reseated, and presented with a cup of mocha-with-soya, all before the door opened to admit the next client, who was that Annabel person. I think it would have been perfectly fair to allow Josephine and Annabel to have left, or at the very least, to have interviewed them first and set them on their way, and I told D.S. Nasir this in no uncertain terms when she called me to the interview room sometime later.

From my vantage point in the chair closest to the door, any other client must pass my seat in order to get to theirs. Each of the stylists, too, passes this spot often, as they beetle to and fro, and little Lily pitter-patters around like Mrs Tiggywinkle with her broom, swishing it around everyone's feet and apologising every time she bashes the brush into someone's shoe, which happens more often than you might expect, considering the girl can *see*. Even Flora, at times, must pass my seat, on the occasions when she ventures into the salon space to relay a message or ask a question of one of the stylists.

Besides all this typical footfall inside the main body of the salon, I also have a good awareness of traffic in and out of the salon door, especially at this time of year when each new arrival or departure blows a gale around my ankles. Even though my back is to the door and the reception desk, the draught alerts me effortlessly to any activity regardless of whether I *hear* anything or not. Thus, I remain fully tuned in to all the comings and goings, unless I am parked at the wash-basin with my head being pummelled with soapy water, and aside from the few minutes in which my hair was being rigorously soaped, Robert J. Robertson could most certainly not have arrived in the salon without my notice.

I could also recall a reasonably accurate schedule of people's movements within the salon, barring the irregular yet frequent passage of the stylists back and forth behind my seat. By this, I mean, one client arrived shortly after I was seated. Another, a few minutes later, was escorted straight from the waiting area to the basins, to be washed. Phyllis, beyond the mirror, was instructed towards the sinks before the other was finished, and both escorted back to the styling chairs within a minute or two of each other. Phyllis, I know, returned to her same seat opposite me, as I would recognise her sneeze anywhere, and she always has a little sneezing fit after a hair wash. We don't know why this occurs; she is not allergic to the shampoo, so we suspect it's that the water gets up her nose. As the two were seated, so the client to my right-hand side was taken off for a wash—not Josephine; the one before Josephine. Phyllis and Josephine really must be discounted from the inquiries, and I do not say this merely on the basis that they are friends of mine.

"Mrs Smith?" Alice's voice jolted me from my thoughts. "Are you all right?"

I wondered if I had been nodding off, as I had quite forgotten she had returned from her interview, which was remiss of me. I should have been interrogating her and trying to speed things along, not drifting off in some daydream.

"Yes, yes, I am managing perfectly well, thank you dear, although it's not very *exciting*, all this sitting around waiting, is it?" I batted at the air with my hand. "I was just having a little rest. Is Flora still here?"

Flora, Alice informed me, had dashed off towards the lavatories just about the same time as Alice had come towards us, looking quite ill. Finbury had tried to stop her, but she had brushed him aside and shoved her way through the door to the ladies', allowing it to swing shut behind her, in Finbury's face.

"I think she was going to be sick." Alice said, theatrically. "I do hope she got there in time. Whatever did you say to her?"

I blanched at that, not a little put out that Alice had so hastily concluded it must have been something I had said that had caused Flora to feel ill.

"Did you say something about her and Robert?"

I gave myself a little shake and forced my thoughts back to the conversation with Flora. We'd been chatting quite nicely, on the whole. What had I said? Ah, that was it. "No. Well, yes, but that wasn't it. The last thing I said, just as I heard you pit-patting towards us, was just as I said to you: one amongst us must be the murderer. I suppose she hadn't thought of that." Or perhaps she hadn't thought that I would notice. "How did you get on with that lovely Detective Sergeant? Do tell me everything, or I fear I shall fall asleep and develop a terrible crick in my neck."

Chapter Seven

Alice, perhaps unsurprisingly, did not tell me very much, having been instructed not to gossip until everyone had been interviewed. However, having ascertained that I was as comfortable as could be expected, given the circumstances, she did skip off to fetch me another cup of tea, whilst D.S. Nasir, D.I. Nelson, and Dougal Rufus Finbury took a moment to confer on the pavement outside the salon door and thus beyond everyone's earshot.

With all three police officers momentarily detained, the murmur in the salon rose to an excited hubbub as people hastily compared theories in hushed but feverish whispers. Phyllis, taking advantage of the situation, shuffled her chair until it lined up with the space between our dividing mirrors and hissed through the gap until I turned my head accurately towards her.

"Where are you Phyl? Am I looking the right way? It's terribly difficult to pinpoint you amongst all this hoohah."

"A little to your right; you're staring at the mirror still. That's it, I'm just here! But now you've found me, turn your head a little so you can hear me properly. Listen. Claude said there was a lot of blood. He also said he was in the cupboard this morning, as he needed to get the potions ready for the client before me, and for my tint. I do like how he calls it potions as if we are in a witch's lair, don't you? About ten-thirty, I think he said, after his first client left, anyway, and then again after the one before me. His last before lunch, that is, so he thinks maybe around eleven-forty-five, at a guess. He was garbling a bit." She took a little breath and gave a funny half-giggle as if she realised she might be garbling too, but I did appreciate her cramming in as much information as she could, and I'm quite used to her.

"Go on, Phyl, go on."

"He's worried about what this might do to his business. He didn't have anything good to say about Robertson, I can tell you. Said the man's a cheat and a swindler while he was tidying up my hair, and it didn't sound as if they were on friendly terms *at all*. Do you think Claude might have killed him? I wouldn't think it of Claude, but he is very tall so you never can tell. He didn't go into details, so I'll see what else I can find out. Maud said she was here at lunchtime, with Alice."

I knew about Maud and Alice already, of course, so it was old news but I guessed Phyllis had more to say on the matter, or she wouldn't have brought it up.

She didn't let me down.

"They were here from about twelve-forty-five, Maud thinks, but she said they didn't see Mr Robertson come in. They'd been for lunch together, and finished up early. She hasn't seen Alice for weeks, and had been looking forward to catching up with all her news, so she isn't very happy about this as you can imagine. It was too cold outside to do any window shopping after they'd had lunch, so they changed their minds about it and then Maud needed a wee, so they nipped straight back here instead. Alice let them in. She'd been crying, you know? Her eyes were all red when we got here so I don't know if they'd had an upset. Maud had a spill down her front." She lowered her voice even further at this, so I guessed she didn't want Maud to overhear.

I wriggled a little closer in my chair to catch her next words.

"So maybe she'd taken it out on poor Alice? Still dabbing at the wet patch, she was, and I said not to worry as the hairdryer would see to it. You know how Maud is. They all have keys, you know? All the stylists. So any one of them could have popped in over lunch—oops, here comes Claude!" She stopped whispering and there was a soft retreating scrape as she scooted her chair back to where it should be. She is remarkably agile for seventy-five, although if I had her vision, I would be scooting around the place on my chair too. Heaven forbid I try it with my eyes, though; you never know what chaos I could cause colliding with things.

Still, I was pleased we'd had a few moments to connect, even if it had been cut short before I could say much to her in return. I sat back in my chair and replayed her words in my mind, sifting through to see if she had said anything important.

Did Phyl mean Maud had been crying? Or Alice? Alice was still away in the staffroom fetching that tea, so I couldn't ask her. Although I didn't know how that was working out if the officers were trying to conduct interviews in the staffroom but I supposed they had to make allowances.

It would, I decided, be most useful if I could get a moment with Claude. Or Gordon. Or even Bobby-Jo. I needed to follow up Phyllis's bombshell about Claude not liking the dead delivery man very much, and determine whether Bobby-Jo knew if Gordon or any of the others held any grudges against Robert J. Robertson, too. Or if any of them would admit to being on the premises when everyone else was not, or could offer any more insight as to who might have bundled the man into the broom cupboard and clonked him one. I'd need to find out more from Alice about exactly how long she and Maud had been in the salon at lunchtime, as well as which of them had been crying, as that would certainly narrow the window of opportunity for a killer to strike, one way or another.

I swivelled my chair slowly from side to side by pushing against the floor with my foot, and then I had an idea and stopped.

With Alice safely out of the way, fetching that tea from wherever she was able, I feigned a nasty coughing fit.

Just as I had hoped, two somebodies rushed to my side in concern. Claude rested a hand on my shoulder and I knew at once it was he, but with all the rush of footsteps, I couldn't be sure who it was who'd come with him. All was revealed as soon as Gordon called to Lily to buck up and get me a glass of water in that lovely deep baritone of his. I smiled inwardly at the success of my little ruse, all the while pretending the tickle in my throat was bothersome and genuine.

"You okay there Mrs S.?" Claude said, kneading my shoulder with his fingertips. I coughed again a couple of times for good measure and spluttered a little as Gordon pressed a glass of lukewarm water into my hands.

"Is she all right?" Lily's voice quavered like the wings of a butterfly trapped in a window and I waved her away to sit down, flapping at the air with my free hand but not finding her within reach.

"Goodness me, yes, don't worry, it's just a little tickle. You go and sit somewhere and stop worrying. Claude and Gordon will mind me for a minute, won't you dears? I'm sure this will all be over soon, don't you worry." I was quite proud of the way in which I ensured the two men would loiter for a few more moments, if I do say so.

Lily padded away; her footsteps soft and fading fast. The poor lamb; this must have all been a terrible shock to her, I should think, and I was a little worried that her mother still hadn't arrived, as it felt like a good while since Dougal Finbury had telephoned for her to come.

Claude and Gordon did fuss a bit, so I had to quickly find the line between convincing them I needed their presence and alleviating their alarm, but after a minute or two I managed to calm them enough to scatter some casual questions into the mix.

"Do either of you know what is happening? Will we be able to leave anytime soon, only my poor Dennis will be beginning to fret, and it is very nearly his dinner time, you know? And he might not remember to feed poor Amity if I'm not there to remind him." It was a little exaggeration of the truth, as Dennis is good like that and would almost certainly remember. Besides, Amity would remind him with a little nudge of her nose against his hand, if he forgot. She always seems to know when it's time for her dinner. Claude and Gordon have a little poodle and they are very much Dog Lovers, so a little mention of Amity was well-placed to appeal to their sympathies.

Claude was being perfectly sympathetic already, of course, but it's always useful to play one's hand well.

"Are they getting close to discovering which of us is the culprit?" I gave a tiny chuckle, just the right combination of nerves and sobriety. "Have they spoken to you yet?" I knew, of course, that Claude had been the first into the makeshift interview room, although D.S. Nasir had detained him within for only ten minutes before releasing him into the room and calling in Flora, and that was before the body had even been removed, so maybe that was just a preliminary inquiry and they'd talk to him again anyway. Gordon, I deduced, would be summoned next, as he was the only one of the stylists who had not yet been interviewed, and then that would be all the staff, if we discount poor Lily, who was not a real staff member and lower down the pecking order, one might suppose.

Nonetheless, I suspected she would be bumped to the top of the list just as soon as her mother arrived, as that's what I would have done in D.S. Nasir's shoes, and she did seem to be a very practical woman with a lot of common sense. I also had the distinct notion, by this time, that D.S. Nasir was deliberately leaving me until last, in order that I could continue to observe, unnoticed, the clever girl, because any time she came back into the salon, she patted my arm and leant close to my ear to whisper, "Are you holding up there, Mrs Smith? Keep your ears open, won't you."

It made me feel most important, I can tell you. I vowed to myself that I would not let her down.

"Yes, sort of," Gordon said, which I took in answer to the latter of my string of questions. People do tend to answer the last question first, if presented with a sequence, I've noticed.

I wonder if there has been any research into why that may be so. I wasn't entirely clear about what he meant, though, as I didn't think he'd had his turn in the firing line, so to speak.

"And no," added Claude, but before I could hazard a guess as to which of the questions he was providing an answer, the salon door eased open and the cold air swirled into the room once more and the three police officers entered, chattering to each other in two low voices and one high-pitched loudmouth.

"They didn't give much away," Claude whispered hurriedly. "I was here until about twelve-fifteen, and no one thinks he came in during the morning."

"Everyone went in and out of the cupboard sometime before lunch," Gordon added in rapid-fire hushed tones. "Well, most of us, anyway. He wasn't there before lunch, that's for sure. I went in only minutes before I went off, to throw in some soiled towels and an apron. I would have noticed."

"When did you go for lunch?" I whispered back, clutching at his hand to keep him there.

"About twenty to twelve, I should think. I was done early, so made the most of it. Was in the pub by five to, with a plate of chips on the way for me and a BLT for Claude, although I'd managed to have a good bite of that before he showed up." He laughed lightly and I expect they exchanged one of those soppy glances my Dennis used to give me. We'd stopped looking at each other like that long before I lost my vision, although we are still very fond of each other and he does show affection in other ways.

I waited for Gordon to say more about what he'd ordered for lunch, because I could smell a hint of beer on his breath, but he didn't elaborate. Maybe he was worried I might think it unprofessional, but one drink at lunchtime never hurt and I wouldn't judge him for that. I rather like a tipple myself, especially at this time of year when one appreciates a hot toddy to warm oneself on a cold day, or a nip of sherry after dinner. In summertime, I'm quite partial to a sip of rosé. Dennis prefers a hearty red but red wine gives me heartburn so I do tend to stick to the lighter wines, these days, or a nice gin and tonic.

It would be easy enough for even someone as incompetent as Finbury to verify Gordon's and Claude's lunch breaks; he'd only need to ask in the pub and check the till receipts, and I doubted even Dougal Rufus Finbury could mess *that* up.

"And I was only back a few minutes before you arrived, if you remember?" Gordon said, after a few seconds pause in which I think they thought one of the police officers might come along and stop us talking. "I said hello to you in the waiting area as you came in. You were with Phyllis, and Claude had just taken your coats. He'd got back a minute or two after me as he'd popped to the newsagent on the way. He'd only just locked the door when the clock chimed and Flora opened it again, and there you were, on the doorstep with Phyllis. He gave your coats to me, you know, because I was just going off to hang mine, and I'll bet you thought he was such a good host, hanging them for you!" Gordon laughed quietly. "Oops, here they come, better scoot off." He released my hand, and the shadows brightened fractionally as he stepped out of the light and scurried off as a pair of squeaking shoes advanced upon us.

"I do hope—"

We'd all been firmly instructed not to confer, but dear Claude is a quick thinker as well as an exceptional stylist and salon owner, and he cut off Doofus Finbury almost as soon as he'd opened his silly little mouth.

"Mrs Smith just took a little turn. I'm just sitting here with her while Alice fetches her a drink. It might be a good idea to hurry things along, don't you think, before anyone faints from hunger or boredom? I'm quite sure we don't *all* need to be here. Perhaps you could ask your colleague when my clients might be permitted to leave, there's a good chap."

"Could we have a word with you next, Lily?" the Detective Sergeant called from the desk, much in the manner of one calling a patient at the dentist, and causing me to grab onto Claude's arm in dismay.

"Is she old enough to be interviewed without her mother?" I asked him, loud enough for Finbury to hear, given that he was standing close enough that I could smell his cigarettes and deduce he'd had one in the few minutes in which he stood outside on the pavement with his superiors and I'd like to know what they thought of that. "They really ought to wait, don't you think? She's only just seventeen, Alice says. Have you taken that into account? Have you?"

Judging by the huff emitting from Finbury, I wondered for a moment if he hadn't realised, but D.S. Nasir stepped in to save him, by calling out, "That'll be her mum now, I should think. Flora, could you let her in please? Lock the door behind her. Thank you."

For about the ninety-ninth time since we'd been locked in, the door was unlocked, opened, and relocked, and the high-pitched, panic-ridden voice of a harassed and angry woman filled the salon.

"What have you done with my Lily? She has rights, you know! You can't just keep her locked up in here for hours all day without food or a responsible adult, you know? I'll be having a ..."

The rush of running feet and muffling of the objections indicated that Lily's relief at seeing her mother overrode any embarrassment about the woman's hysterical complaints.

"Mum!"

"Lils!"

What followed was a waterfall of sobbing, another huffing sigh from Finbury, and the gentle voice of Detective Sergeant Nasir, saying, "I'll just give you a minute, then if you could both pop in here with me ..."

A moment later, three pairs of feet shuffled away towards the staff room, followed by the heavier footfall I had deduced must belong to the Detective Inspector.

In the salon, there fell another of those pregnant pauses while the rest of us gathered our thoughts and I wondered whether Claude minded about not being considered a responsible adult by his work experience's mother.

As there was no sound from Finbury, I couldn't be entirely sure whether he had retreated to the staffroom with the D.I., D.S. Nasir, Lily, and Lily's mother, although during the other interviews, he'd been left in the salon to guard the rest of us and ensure we didn't confer, and I saw no reason to think otherwise so I assumed he was still with us, sitting somewhere in merciful silence for a change.

I'd gathered from Claude's hurried precis that Flora had spent most of the last hour or so stationed in her usual spot behind the desk, aside from that brief interlude when she'd been delegated to sit here with me. The salon's five captive clients, he'd said, had been mainly restricted to our chairs and the stylists allowed to attend to the clients as necessary, but otherwise relegated to sitting quietly on the bench in the waiting area, flicking pointlessly through old magazines and worrying about things. By the time I got hold of Claude, with my faked coughing fit, our imposed agreement not to talk was wearing very thin, and much of our initial tolerance was beginning to fray as the time ticked slowly by.

Beside me, Josephine complained loudly about having left her dog alone for too long, and I called out to her that Amity would, too, be beginning to fret were I not home soon. Of course, being a guide dog, Amity is trained not to fret, but even so, one does worry about one's responsibilities.

Annabel had needed to call a neighbour at five to three to arrange collection of her children from school, and although she has one of those terribly posh voices that led me to suppose she has the kind of pointy cheekbones one imagines in the movies, she was becoming increasingly flustered about being home in time to feed them and get them off to bed, which was something Bobby-Jo started to worry about too, once Annabel said it.

"At this rate," Bobby-Jo mumbled in a loud faux-whisper from the other side of the dividing mirrors, "even Santa will have been and gone before we get home." We still had almost a week until Christmas Eve but I took her point. At that, she'd informed Finbury in a louder but more resigned tone that she supposed she'd better sort someone to collect her little darlings from their after school club, and Finbury had huffed away to retrieve her telephone.

"Not that one! Do I look like the kind of person who would have a pink sparkly phone cover? Do I?"

A few moments later, by which time Finbury must have found the correct device from the collection on the reception desk, Bobby-Jo had moaned loudly into the telephone that, "Some idiot policeman is holding us captive even though it's blindingly obvious—even to an imbecile—I hadn't even been on the premises when—" Bobby-Jo stopped talking abruptly, and Claude stifled a chortle before bending close to my ear and relaying in a whisper laden with undisguised glee that Finbury had snatched the phone from Bobby-Jo's hand.

Finbury then barked an order to the person on the other end that he was an officer of the law. "You will be cautioned if you repeat anything Bobby-Jo just told you, so could you kindly collect any relevant children belonging to Bobby-Jo and keep them occupied until further notice?" Dougal Rufus had not been one of the popular boys during his school years, and it seemed apparent even to an almost-blind old woman that he had done little to improve his social skills in more recent years.

Claude was still standing behind me, both hands resting on my shoulders, rubbing knots from my collar bone, and chuckling to himself in silent tremors.

Alice, having returned with a cup of tea for herself just as D.S. Nasir had led Lily to the staffroom, had made one for me too, which was convenient given the little white lies we'd told about her nipping off to get me one, so despite an inevitability that it would only trigger another trip to the ladies', I took it gratefully.

"Alice," I whispered as she set the tea into my hands, "do you think you may be able to distract P.C. Finbury while I continue to chat with Claude for a few more minutes? We all need a change of scene and if we pool our resources, perhaps we'll get to the bottom of this sooner rather than later."

"Gotcha, Mrs Smith," she whispered back. She patted my leg, and off she skedaddled.

Claude sank onto the chair Alice had dragged over what seemed like several hours before but was probably not that long at all, and the air left the seat with a satisfying squoosh as he sat, merging with his sigh into one long sound.

"I am terribly sorry for all this inconvenience," he said heavily, reaching over to squeeze my hand—the one that was not holding the cup of tea.

"It is quite as much of an inconvenience to you," I said. "More, I should imagine."

"Blinkin' infuriating man, that Robertson," he said, with bitterness I wasn't sure was entirely warranted just because the man had been careless enough to get himself killed in Claude's cleaning cupboard. "I'm so sorry Mrs S., that was terribly unprofessional, but honestly, this is just so ... so ..."

"Inconvenient?" I said, with a smile. "It's really not your fault, Claude." I stopped, stilling his hand on mine. "Unless it is? Did you kill him, Claude?" I was sure to keep my voice light, to let him know I didn't think for a moment he had, even though it was, of course, perfectly possible. I listened to a documentary once, which expanded on the premise that it is, indeed, perfectly possible for *anyone* to commit murder, given the right set of circumstances. You really do never know. "Tell me about the man. Was he a regular delivery driver? Did you know him well?"

Chapter Eight

In hushed and hurried fragments whispered furtively between overly-cheerful, normal-voiced, banal chitchat that led me to deduce Finbury was lurking nearby, Claude told me Robert J. Robertson was both a regular delivery man, and quite disliked. He made deliveries to the salon approximately three or four times a month, bringing supplies of consumables such as shampoo, conditioners, treatments, and colours as well as equipment such as hairdryers and brushes. The kind of things ordered from the hairdressing suppliers, but not such mundane things as stocks of lavatory paper or teabags, which were ordered through and delivered by an entirely different company.

Into these whispered snippets of information, Claude interjected phrases such as "thieving", "pinched", "smarmy", "not to be trusted", and referred to the dead man as a cheating-something-or-other I don't care to repeat. He finished up with an emphatic, "Look, Mrs S., I really don't like to speak ill of the dead, and it's not a very charitable thing to say, but I won't be sorry that this ... *incident* will, at least, keep him away from my girls."

By 'my girls', I concluded he meant the girls working in the salon. Alice and Flora, to be specific.

"Thieving?" I whispered back, deciding that Alice and Flora had covered much of 'smarmy' and 'cheating' in their depiction of the man, and my snatched moments of time talking with Claude would be better served by focusing on this new information.

"Hand-in-the-till kind of bloke. Had to watch him."

"You caught him stealing from the till?"

"Not exactly," he amended, still whispering. "Some deliveries were short. Missing a bottle of shampoo here and a canister of Moroccan oil there. Not for himself, shouldn't think, not by the state of his hair." His hand trembled on mine and I interpreted the shudder than ran through him as disapproval of the man's hair maintenance, or lack thereof. Perhaps he had sported a particularly unstylish thatch of hair, although Flora hadn't said anything about that.

I was longing to ask Claude what was wrong with the man's hair, but time was of the essence and it didn't seem the most important thing, especially when one takes into consideration that Claude himself is perfectly bald-headed, so hardly in a position to judge, even if he is the finest hairstylist in Little Wittering. Instead, I squeezed his hand reassuringly and asked what else had been stolen.

"Small things. Money missing from coat pockets. An infuser. One of those nice vanilla ones. Pods from the coffee machine. Whatever he could get out without being noticed. Always took the empty boxes away, he did, if you get my drift."

"Ah. Not actually empty, then?"

"Exactly. Not actually empty. Couldn't prove it was him. Never caught him at it. Seemed too convenient, things always going missing on the days he showed up. Had to watch him."

I let the information settle for a moment, wondering whether recurrent petty theft was enough to kill someone for.

"Alice said he was a cheat in love, too. Poor dear girl." I decided to file away the thievery for the moment and see what else I could get out of Claude before Doofus Finbury broke up our little conflab.

"Caused quite the rumpus. Alice was teary for days. Fought with Flora over it. Handbags at dawn, dah-ling. Quite the show. Gordy and I had to intervene; pull them apart and put them in separate corners for time out."

I allowed myself a small chuckle at the idea of Claude and Gordon plucking up each girl by the scruff of her neck and dropping them into separate areas in the manner of one splitting up fighting kittens, or one of those choreographed wrestling matches Dennis and I used to watch at Butlins. We were treated to so much wonderful entertainment on those annual summer breaks; quite the cabaret each evening, and me in my finest ball gowns, too, so we could have a dance.

"Just not in front of the customers, please, ladies, I had to tell them," Claude said, wistfully, and the memories of ball gowns and Butlins vanished as he patted my shoulder sympathetically, and I got the distinct impression that Claude had also lapsed into a little daydream as he remembered the scenes of Flora's and Alice's altercations. "Although they did use some marvellously inventive insults. Quite splendid," he'd added in the voice he uses when he is showing a client how wonderful their new hairdo looks.

The tones of admiration in Claude's whispered regaling suggested he'd quite enjoyed the drama of the catfight between the girls, and I was suddenly quite certain he'd even encouraged it somewhat, even if he had disapproved of the disruption to the smooth-running of his salon.

"Gordy and I laughed about it, after, when we were alone, but it was not the kind of behaviour we can allow on the shop floor. They were only seconds away from claws and biting, at the worst of it. Why anyone would fight over that smarmy creep was beyond us, Mrs S., quite beyond us."

I don't know whether it's relevant at all, but I don't recall whether I have mentioned that Claude and Gordon are 'together', if you know what I mean. I am glad that kind of thing has become normalised. It does make it so much more pleasant than all that sneaking around that the likes of Barney White had to do back in my day, pretending to ask girls to dances, when anyone could see he had designs on Clive Goodson. He used to follow him around like a lovesick puppy. I could quite envisage them dissecting the details of the fight as they sat together over a beer. Claude and Gordon, that is, not Barney and Clive. Clive moved to Woking in about 1983, I do believe, and Barney went off to join the army, and that was that.

Whether Claude had more to say about Robert J. Robertson I can't say, as he had chuckled a little too loudly as he remembered Flora and Alice bashing each other with handbags, and the waft of cigarette-breath and the piercing squeak of flat-footed strides heading in our direction told me our tête-a-tête was about to be interrupted.

Sure enough, seconds after the cigarette-reek reached my nose, Finbury put on his most jumped-up tones and I imagine he pulled himself up to his full height, although he never was tall, and Claude is over six foot, and said, "What's going on here then?"

I have to admit I needed to stifle a little giggle behind my hand because I am quite sure he learned that line from a cartoon show on the television and I wondered for the umpteenth time how he had ever graduated from police training college and why he wasn't sitting in a corner somewhere wearing one of those conical pointed dunce's hats.

"Did you bend your knees and bounce up and down as you said that, Dougal Rufus?" I said the words as sweetly as I could, although only within the privacy of my head. Even though I didn't speak the jibe aloud, I felt instantly remorseful. No teacher should ever be so unkind as to tease their pupils, and while he may be in his thirties and I may be long-retired, I am not the kind of person who is a bully.

"Now then, now then—" I started to say instead, and had to bite down hard on the inside of my lip to contain another chuckle and remind myself to be the better person. "Claude was just trying to cheer me up. Are we going to be here for very much longer? I do need to go home and get my Dennis his tea. I'm really not very confident that he will manage to produce anything palatable by himself, and I certainly would prefer him not to set fire to the microwave again."

"Perhaps you'd like another cup of tea while you are waiting, Mrs Smith?" Finbury said, which shows you how lacking he is in observational skills.

I lifted the cup I had balanced on my lap, and drew it back and forth in front of my chest, taking care not to slop it. "If you used those eyes of yours, you would be able to tell I am currently partaking of what must be about my fifty-seventh cup of tea. I do believe I shall need to visit the ladies' again quite soon. Also, I should very much like to speak with my friend Phyllis, if you don't mind?"

He told me, of course, that he did mind, and then he told Claude to come along and stop talking to the other witnesses.

"Have you forgotten that I can't see? I am hardly a stellar witness," I lied, hoping he would take my words at face value and allow me a little freedom. "Besides, I am getting awfully stiff, and my joints will soon lock up terribly painfully if I am not permitted to move."

He huffed and sighed and shuffled about, causing his shoes to squeak most unpleasantly against the floor. I'm sure I could hear the cogs whirring in his little brain as he weighed up the benefits of keeping me confined to my chair versus the formal complaints I may register with his superiors were I not allowed to stretch my legs.

"Alice," he called, as if she were far away. "Take Mrs Smith here for a walk around the salon. But do not—" He leaned in close and the whiff of Marlboros tickled the back of my throat and my cough was not at all faked this time around. "—*talk* to anyone. I will be keeping an eye on you."

"I will need to speak to Alice, so she can guide me. I would really prefer not to trip over anything and break my neck. It would inconvenience you and dear Claude most terribly if there were to be another death on the premises in such a short space of time. Now, take this for me, so I can get out of this blessed chair." I swallowed down the last of my tea and pushed the cup towards the cigarette-scented shadow, until it met resistance, and then, counting to three in my head, I let go of the handle.

"Oof!"

There was no clatter of china on tiles, so I presumed he had safely made the catch. I shuffled forwards in the chair, gripping the arms tightly as I used them for leverage to propel myself from the seat. My foot landed, entirely by accident, of course, on Finbury's shoe and he jumped backwards out of the way, clearing the air around me once more. "Alice? Alice dear, are you here? Where is my cane? There do appear to be some unexpected obstacles on the salon floor and I will be much safer once I have my cane in my hands to help me avoid such obstructions."

The hand that took my elbow was large and firm and belonged not to Alice but to dear Claude. "Two steps to your right Mrs S.; I'll hand you to Alice then get your cane. There you are now." He squeezed my arm gently and spun me around a hundred and eighty degrees. Alice's slim, warm hand slipped into the crook of my arm, and Claude let go. A moment later he put the cane into my other hand, wrapping my fingers carefully around the top, and with another little squish of my hand, relinquished me into Alice's care.

"First things first," I announced. "I think we should visit the ladies' room. If you would be so kind." I didn't need to go, but Dougal Rufus, I was quite certain, would not dare to follow us there.

"I ... you ... you can't ..." he blustered, and again, I was forced to bite my lip.

"Can't what? Dougal? I trust you are not trying to prevent a seventy-four-year-old woman with artificial hips and a weak bladder from visiting the lavatory?"

"I ... well ... I ... but ..."

"Dear Alice, perhaps we could pop along to the staffroom first, and clear it with that *lovely Detective Sergeant*?" I put as much emphasis on the words 'lovely' and 'detective' and 'sergeant' as one can without sounding constipated, and it seemed to do the trick because Finbury made no further attempts to protest, and Alice guided me quietly to the ladies' room, neither of us speaking a word.

Once the door to the lobby was closed firmly behind us, Alice burst into muffled giggles. "His face was so red, Mrs Smith! If only you could have seen ..." She let go of my arm and her hair brushed against my hands as she doubled over. "I know this is the most horrendous day, and I really shouldn't be laughing, but ... his face! You really should have ..." Again, her words were lost as she tried to quash her laughter.

I let her laugh for a few moments, glad for the light moment, and eventually she pulled herself together, straightened herself up, and took a deep breath somewhere level with my ear.

"Do you really need the loo?" she whispered.

I supposed it would be sensible to go while I was there, so I tapped my way into the cubicle and fumbled around until I found the bolt, did my business, and repeated the fumble to unlock the door. With the benefit of running water and the blowing of the hand drier, we managed to snatch several more minutes of forbidden conversation and I quickly followed up the comment Flora had made earlier, when she was telling me about her unfortunate nighttime encounter with Robert J Robertson.

"Was he—" I hesitated for a second, thinking of how best to phrase the question. "Was he ever *rough*?" I groped for the button on the hand-drier and pressed it again, to keep the noise up. "In the bedroom department, that is? I'm sorry to ask you this, dear, but something Flora said ..." I allowed the words to trail off, letting her make her own inference.

She was quiet for a moment and the little clicking sounds suggested she was tapping her fingernails against my cane, which she was minding for me while I dried my hands. When she did speak, it was so quiet I had to strain to catch it over the whooshing air. "He could be; yes. He didn't like it much when I said I wasn't in the mood. He could be quite forceful, sometimes."

The drier finished and she tucked my cane into my hands and tucked her hand into the bend of my elbow.

"He wasn't a very nice man, Mrs Smith, you must remember that." She said it so clearly and firmly it left me a little shocked, the shy mumble of just earlier dissipated, as if there was an important message there I needed to remember.

A minuscule shudder ran up my spine.

Chapter Nine

As Alice guided me back to the salon floor, it seemed we'd missed a brief moment of excitement. The air was cooler and, towards the doorway onto the street, the low chatter of three female voices drifted to my ears.

"I see, yes. Of course. Thank you."

"Goodbye now, Lily. We'll be in touch, if we need anything more. Try not to worry. Get her home for a good meal and a good night's sleep," came the Detective Sergeant's reassuring tones, answered by a feeble, "Thank you Detective," from Lily's girlish voice.

The door closed; the lock clicked; the air settled once more. Lily, it seemed, had been allowed to leave. D.S. Nasir and D.I. Nelson must be making progress.

Further into the main body of the salon, the deep voice of the Detective Inspector rose above the low hum of the others' mumbling and murmuring. "Why don't we see if we can get some sandwiches sent in from the hotel?"

I couldn't tell to whom he had directed this suggestion, but there was a rumble of consent that seemed unanimous, although accompanied by some more grumbling about being held hostage, which you would think would be quite an exciting experience, but in reality was very boring and quite uncomfortable, even though it was only about five o'clock, and many of us would have been here until this time even if things had progressed in the normal and uneventful fashion one expects from an afternoon in Claude's hair salon.

The proposal of sandwiches quickly agreed on, the Detective Inspector instructed Flora to telephone the hotel or the café—"You choose, I'm sure you can manage to sort it out. Phone around if you need to."—and order in a platter of sandwiches. "Some ham and some cheese? That suit everyone?" he asked the room, and was met with communal assent.

"Could we have crisps, too?" someone—I think it was Bobby-Jo—suggested tentatively.

"I suppose that would be all right. Flora?"

"On it, Detective. I'll ask for a selection of flavours, shall I?" she replied, and her voice sounded significantly cheerier at the thought of several packs of cheese-and-onion than it had when she'd been telling me all about Robert J., which was quite telling, don't you agree?

I told Alice, quite loudly, for the benefit of Finbury, that I should like to stroll about the room for a few minutes while awaiting the arrival of the sandwiches, to loosen up the joints and keep the blood circulating, and I was sure it would be all right with the police officers, because at my age, it's imperative to keep moving, you know?

"I don't see why not," the Inspector's voice boomed. I was already warming to him, although we'd hardly spoken. He had quite the air of authority and calm and emitted a reassuring sense of the type of man who was good at getting things done. I suppose that's why he holds the position of Inspector. I suspected he, too, was grateful for the little interval in proceedings, and I imagined him having a stretch of his back and easing his neck back from side to side as he took advantage of the reprieve from the staffroom, although of course I had no idea what he might look like so it was difficult to picture him stretching. Perhaps the man didn't stretch at all, although I would certainly have taken advantage of the interval in proceedings to do so, and in my mind, a Burt Reynolds lookalike stroked his moustache, tipped a gangster-style hat, and displayed an inch of muscular midriff, and I smiled to myself at the daydream although I doubt Dennis would have approved very much of my little lapse into such a fantasy. I attempted to shake Burt Reynolds out of my mind by replacing him with a brief notion of us all having a little Pilates session before the interviewing recommenced, all stretching together, but I am quite sure that Dougal Finbury would not have approved of the suggestion, whatever D.S. Nasir or D.I. Burt Reynolds-Nelson might have thought, so I kept it to myself and of course it didn't happen.

As Alice and I began our promenade around the room, the other clients took full advantage of their eyesight, with each one greeting me as I approached, starting with Josephine, who we got to first.

"Are you coping all right, Sal?" Josephine has strong Liverpudlian vowels, so even had Alice not informed me it was she who was seated beside me in the salon, or had Josephine not greeted me on her way in, I would have known it was she as soon as she spoke. "It really is too much, isn't it? I do hope we get out of here soon."

"I simply can't imagine why they are keeping us all here," I said, in my firmest teacher's voice. "They can't possibly think we are responsible, when we arrived after the man was killed."

"Are you quite sure? What if he was killed while we were sitting here?"

"I am quite certain. I would have heard him arrive and I would have heard the scuffle."

Alice tugged gently at my arm to keep me moving forwards, mindful, I suppose, of the police officers' watchful eyes.

"No one," I said quietly towards Josephine's voice, "is bashed about the head without some kind of scuffle, or at least an audible thump. I would also think one would shout, wouldn't you? And if you had heard anything untoward or out of place, you would have mentioned it to Gordon, just as I would have commented to Alice. I think any one of us would have turned to our stylist and asked if they had heard a strange noise, don't you think? You and I," I added, for good measure, "are especially adept at identifying unexpected thumps. It's part of the job."

"I'm sure you're right," she said, and Alice and I rounded the corner to pass in front of the basins.

"As is Phyllis," I added over my left shoulder, accidentally swinging my cane into the base of the mirrored divider in my haste to reassure my colleague and salon-neighbour.

"Basin steps to your right, Mrs Smith," Alice said, quite unnecessarily, given that she had hold of my right arm and walked slowly between me and the steps, but I suppose she was making it quite clear exactly where in the room we were located. She really is very good at guiding the visually impaired and that is most certainly not a skill everyone possesses, I can tell you.

"Mind you don't catch Gran's bag with your cane now," she announced, proving the point. I was perfectly sure that Maud's bag would be stashed neatly out of the way, and was no imminent danger to me whatsoever.

"Hello Sally." Maud's voice was subdued and not at all her cheerful self, which I suppose was to be expected, under the circumstances. "What an unfortunate turn of events this has become. How terribly awful that everyone's afternoon has been so inconvenienced by that awful, awful man. I'm so terribly sorry, Sally, you must be finding it most tiresome, and without that lovely dog of yours to keep you company, too." Maud is one of those worrywart people who is always apologising, whether or not she has any responsibility for the matters at hand. It can be a little wearing, after a while, but as I mentioned, Maud and I are not close friends so I only have to put up with it on occasion.

I reciprocated her sentiments and asked after her other grandchildren. She has several, and Alice is somewhere in the middle. There are also two great grandchildren and one on the way so that took us the few seconds until Alice guided me on past her grandmother and towards my dear friend Phyllis, who I could smell already. She has been wearing that same delightful lily-of-the-valley scent for years; ever since I stood beside her as she married her beloved Frederick, some fifty-odd years ago; a prettily blushing bride clutching a spray of lily of the valley entwined with baby's breath and some delicate peach-coloured roses. Weddings were quite simple, in our day, but I would suggest they were all the more special for that.

Nowadays, one does get a little *lost* in the excess, don't you agree?

As I approached, her chair gave a faint squeal, followed by a soft groan and a series of creaks. She reached out with her tissue-soft hand and took my arm to anchor me and bring me to a halt. "Sally," she said, in a voice as soft as a summer breeze. "How are you coping with all this palaver? I'm afraid poor Zachary will be most disappointed to have missed us." Zachary is the dashing young waiter with whom we had expected to be having a flirtatious encounter later that afternoon, in the comfort of the hotel lounge, sporting our new hairdos.

Zachary, to be perfectly honest, having been quite unaware of our intentions to partake of the hotel's afternoon tea, would not have missed us at all, and I said this as economically as I could to Phyllis, who said, "Yes, I suppose you are right. Still, it would have been nice," in a wistful sort of way. We hadn't made a reservation, you see. One doesn't really need to. Not even this close to the festive season. This is not a busy town by any stretch of one's imagination, even in December. Especially in December, now I think of it. One tends to prefer somewhere a little more festive, at Christmas, don't you find? A skiing vacation in the Alps, perhaps, or one of those wonderful Northern Lights displays. Not ordinary, rainy Little Wittering.

I had hoped Phyllis would have had something more useful to say in this brief moment of interaction. "Perhaps we could go tomorrow, instead," I told her, as Alice led me on.

"And here's Annabel's chair now; sidestep to your left. That's it. And one more." Alice nudged me gently in the direction she suggested, in order to safely manoeuvre around the next chair.

I can't claim to know Annabel, nor could I dredge up any recollection of anyone by that name, but I am an outgoing kind of person and never mind making a new acquaintance. I chatted to someone at the bus stop one afternoon for so long I invited her in for afternoon tea, in the end, but she said she had to meet the three o'clock train and we never did meet again, I don't think. Besides, when one has been locked inside a hair salon for several hours, one is predisposed to speak with almost anyone if one is given the chance.

"Nice to meet you, Annabel," I said, with a smile. "I don't believe I know you? I am Mrs Smith." I nodded in what I hoped was the direction of her face, although I had no way to determine whether she faced into the room, or towards the wall, in the direction in which the chair must usually face.

There was the faintest rustle of paper as if one might be turning a page in a paperback or slipping a bookmark into place. "Nice to meet you Mrs Smith," Annabel said, in that soft, well-spoken voice. "I've seen you around town."

I sniffed the air delicately, picking up on the distinct smell of hair colouring. "You came in for a colour? I can smell the lotion. Which colour did you choose?"

She told me she was having her roots done, and a nice balayage, and I made a mental note to ask Alice what that meant, with shades of chestnut to complement her natural dirty blonde. I couldn't think why she needed to complement her natural colour if she was getting her roots done and covering up everything natural, but I cast that thought aside and imagined a balayage could be one of those sharp-cut bobs one might expect from the olden days, typically worn with what one used to call alabaster skin tones, although I suspect people don't think about alabaster much these days. Nonetheless, I thought an angular bob and alabaster would go awfully well with the notions I'd had earlier about Annabel's cheekbones, and for the second time that afternoon, I had a sudden longing to reach out and touch someone and see if I couldn't get a better idea about the cheeks and the hair, if nothing about the alabaster.

I decided to ask Alice about it later, and asked Annabel if she was very fed up with all this inconvenience.

She laughed quite cheerfully so perhaps she wasn't quite as angular as I had envisaged, and said not at all because she'd brought along a good book and didn't often get such a long break from her kids, and actually it was almost like a holiday and maybe men should get murdered in cupboards all the time if it gave her an afternoon off from the school run. Then she gasped and laughed again in that funny abbreviated way one does when embarrassed, and said of course she didn't mean that, and it was terrible for the poor man, but it was nice to have a break, nonetheless. At that, I had to re-evaluate my image of her entirely as she didn't seem so posh as I had supposed her to be, which goes to show one can't always tell about a person from the sound of their voice, and then she gave the softest sigh, like a happy cat settling onto one's lap, and rustled the pages again.

I asked her what the book was, but it wasn't anything I'd heard of, and then Alice led me around the corner and I was back at my own seat, resting my hand on the back of it while I caught up with myself and my bearings.

"I think, if you don't mind," I said to Alice, "we could go around again?"

Chapter Ten

With Alice still on my right, and the central quartet of styling chairs to my left, and with Alice's hand tucked into my right arm, and my cane tucked into my left hand, assuming no one had moved within the last few minutes, I would not need to worry about finding my path on the second circuit of the salon. Nonetheless, I hobbled along at the pace of a somnolent snail, giving myself time to think.

In anticipation of Doofus stepping in and prohibiting too many more circuits of the room, I needed to plan my conversations carefully. What did I most need to know?

I replayed my earlier conversation with Alice, thinking about the *Who? Why?* and *When?* The *where* component of the puzzle, at least, was perfectly evident as I don't think anyone had any doubt that Robert J. Robertson had been killed where he lay.

Whilst it was imperative to establish motive, in order to net the killer, it would be more productive to first weed out all those who were not in the right place at the right time, such as Phyllis. With that in mind, you might speculate I had no need to speak to Phyllis. Even had she not entered the salon alongside me, I trust her completely. Phyllis couldn't hurt a fly.

People bandy about that term in a figurative sense, but with Phyllis, I use the term quite literally. She would open every window in the house, even in a freezing January or rainy June thunderstorm, and lure a fly out with a trail of jam rather than trap or kill the little beast, no matter how irritating its buzzing. I must admit I have no such leniency and would squash them in a heartbeat if I could only see to catch the little blighters.

However, Phyllis, I was certain, would be able to divulge some information I was not yet party to, for Phyllis had something useful I was lacking: Phyllis is blessed with exceptional vision, even though she turned seventy-five in March. Phyllis is a woman who notices details. She was a librarian, you see, and librarians, like teachers, must be in possession of proficient observational skills. A librarian must be acutely aware who amongst her customers is likely to have sticky fingers – in both senses of the phrase – or from which alcove the rustling of sweet papers emanates. A librarian must be adept at summing up the characters of those who are most likely to dog-ear pages or conceal a drink in their bag, and must be ready to intervene before calamities arise. Prevention, as they say, is better than cure, and that, Phyllis believes, is a particularly pertinent motto to live by in a library. I must say I am inclined to agree with her on that point. Many a first edition or special issue has been protected from careless readers by a librarian, as she is fond of reminding me. Phyllis is not only blessed with sharp eyes, but also with hearing almost as sharp and finely-tuned as my own. A librarian is also, of course, accustomed to hearing the very faintest of noises and recognising each for what it is. Phyllis, I can assure you, can differentiate between the kind of sneeze that needs a tissue and a handwash from the kind of sneeze that doesn't, at a hundred paces. She may be retired, but she keeps her skills honed for those sticky afternoons on which her great-grandchildren visit, and practices on long train journeys to visit her son in Morecambe.

Of course, Phyllis was seated at the penultimate station of my circumnavigation of the styling consoles, and I would first come again to Josephine. However, as I was confident of Josephine's innocence, and as her position in the salon was the least favourable for the purpose of observation of the crime scene, I simply couldn't think of anything useful to ask her. To the best of my knowledge, she has perfectly adequate eyesight, but when one is facing into the furthest corner of a room, and the action has happened somewhere behind you, on the other side of a protruding partition wall, the sharpest eyesight in the world is of little use.

Aha! I thought, as my cane picked out the base of her chair, *there is something she might know!* "Josephine," I said, as quietly as I could manage while still expecting her to hear me, "what has Gordon had to say about the matter?"

I heard the squeak of her bottom rising from the faux-leather, and sensed her closing in as she rose and bent to my ear. She smelled of the regular salon shampoo and for a fraction of a second I wondered whether it was time for Alice to give my hair its second rinse. I get it washed twice, with a colour, once before and once after, just to be sure, but then I remembered it had already been done, and I suppose I must have had a momentary lapse, what with all the hoohah.

"He said," Josephine whispered, close to my ear so no one else would hear, "the man was a filthy toerag and had his fingers in the till and Claude had complained about him more than once and thank goodness he'd never do the deliveries again. Not to mention how he'd upset our Alice and then Flora too." She interjected one of those huffy little sniffles that are intended only to portray disapproval and have little to do with nasal irritations. "If I didn't know him better, I'd have thought he sounded quite pleased that the poor man is dead. He didn't sound sorry at all, at first, but then he swore quite a bit about the mess and he's terribly worried because he says Claude is in a terrible flap about how it will affect the business, even though you'd never know it. Claude is a beacon of strength, he said, who can keep his showman face on when he needs to. He said poor Claude will hold it together until they get home and then it will be all tears and chocolate, you mark his words."

Alice, during this long, hushed spiel, kept tugging gently on my arm.

I flapped at her a few times to wait a moment, and put my finger to my lips, hoping she would get the message, but then she tugged a little harder and whispered, "Dougal!" in my other ear.

I quickly whispered to Josephine, "Could he have done it?" and she whispered back, "Who?"

I said, "I meant Gordon, but either of them, really?"

"Goodness, I shouldn't think so, but you never can tell, can you? He sounded awfully angry about the man."

Then sausage-breath Doofus's shoes squeaked up behind me and Josephine fell away onto her chair with a *swssh* of air and Alice pulled me on and around in front of the sinks.

"Alice, dear, have you forgotten my second rinse?"

"Oh!" She stopped in her tracks and I imagined her mouth hung open in a moment of panic, just as I am quite certain I felt the weight of her gaze on my hair.

I flashed a grin in her direction, and she said, "We already did it, didn't we? You're having a little joke," in quite a cheery tone. She tapped my arm with her fingers as if she was telling me off, and I was pleased I'd made her smile. "Hello again Gran!" she called, but although her voice was loud and high, it hadn't quite the same cheerfulness and had acquired a somewhat brittle edge, as if the day's events were beginning to catch up with her, and I suddenly realised that what Alice really needed was to give her grandmother a big hug.

"Maud," I said, "I think your granddaughter is feeling a little fragile with all this hoohah, and I think she needs a bit of a cuddle from her granny. Doesn't a cuddle from a granny put everything right, eh love?" I added to Alice, keeping my voice low but no longer bothering to whisper as it's terribly hard work to speak in nothing but whispers for an entire afternoon although I suppose Phyllis, at least, was quite used to that and would be faring admirably.

Maud shuffled up from her seat—she is a bit more agile than me, being some years younger, and a little sprightlier, although she is several pounds heavier than me, according to Phyllis, who has described Maud as "quite plump, but with a pleasant enough face, like a picture book." I think she probably means to say that Maud reminds her of a storybook grandmother, but Phyllis does get a bit muddled with her similes sometimes although that's the only sign that she isn't getting any younger. She's sharp as a pin in every other way.

I rested my hands on the back of Maud's chair, so I wouldn't lose my sense of place, and Alice slipped her hand from my elbow to embrace her grandmother, while I kept my ears pricked for signs of Dougal Finbury creeping up on us to put a stop to it.

"Oh Allie," Maud whispered in a bit of a muffle, although whether the muffling was from emotion or from being buried into Alice's hair, I couldn't tell you. "I do wish we could just go home. I'm so sorry you've had to deal with all this, sweetie. It should never have come to this, although he was a thoroughly unpleasant man."

"Oh Gran," Alice whispered back. "It wasn't your fault. I'm sorry too. This was supposed to be such a lovely treat for you and it's turned into the most horrible day." With that, Alice burst into loud and sniffling sobs and I could feel Maud rocking her back and forth because it made the chair rock back and forth too, as she knocked against it.

"There, there," she kept saying, in that meaningless way one does when one can't solve a situation yet knows one's loved ones are in distress. "There, there."

Luckily, it wasn't Finbury who intervened, but the lovely Detective Sergeant, who said softly, "It's just me, Sally; Sana Nasir. Would you like to take my arm?"

At that moment the phone rang, over at the reception desk, and Flora sounded quite chipper as her voice rose above Alice's sobs and Finbury's advancing huffing. I slipped my hand into the crook of the Detective Sergeant's arm, just as Flora said brightly, "Sandwiches in five, hostages. Let's get this party started."

There was a thin ripple of laughter for the briefest of moments, and someone who was probably Bobby-Jo called back, "Is there wine?" which made everyone laugh some more.

D.S. Nasir said, "Alice, Maud, come along now. Why don't I take Mrs Smith back to her seat while you go and freshen up, Alice, and then I will see Maud next in the interview room over a sandwich or two?"

"How about you just leave me here beside Phyllis for a minute?" I suggested, hopefully. "I can find my way to my seat from Phyl's chair well enough, I'm sure."

I could guess that D.S. Nasir looked from me to Maud, to Alice, and to each of us again in turn, although of course she may not have done so, but her tone of voice and the accompanying weighted pause certainly led me to imagine it was so.

"I think I'll walk with Alice along to the ladies'," she said, after a moment. "And I'll pop back for you once the sandwiches are here, Maud. Are you perfectly sure you can manage without help, Sally? Give Constable Finbury a shout if you realise you are stuck. Straight back to your seat, mind."

I got the distinct feeling she had given me a tiny gift, as I didn't believe she needed to go with Alice and nor should she have left me beside Phyllis, given we were not supposed to be conferring or speculating over the events. I'm not one to question a gift horse, and I shuffled slowly, carefully, from Maud's chair to Phyllis's, with Phyllis cheering me on as if I were a racehorse—or a gift horse—that might keel over at any moment and lose her a hefty stake.

"Three more steps. Left shuffle. There now! Almost here." And then, she too, was on her feet and I have to confess I felt a small thrill of rebellion at having got *three* of Claude's clients up from the shackles of their seats in just a few minutes. Phyllis took one of my hands in each of hers and gave me a little squeeze.

"Phyl," I hissed under my breath, "tell me very fast; what have you *seen*? Did I miss the delivery man? He really didn't come in while we were sat here having our hair done, did he?"

Phyllis, you will recall, had been seated in a styling chair facing towards the door and the reception desk, and while I suspect the mirror blocks much of her view, she would most certainly be curious enough to look up any and every time the door opens. She is the kind of person who likes to know what's what, and she's terribly observant, as I said.

Her reply was instant. "No. Not one single delivery has arrived in all the time we have been here, unless you count the spotty lad who works at Luigi's who popped in with a leaflet about pizzas, or unless I missed anything while I was at the basin having my shampoo and conditioner." She squeezed my hands again and took a breath before she went on. She does talk rather fast, but then I had told her to be quick, so I suppose I did ask for it. "But while I was at the basin, you were at your seat, so you would have heard if he had arrived at that time, and while you were at the basin, I was back here, bundled in my towel and waiting for Lily to fetch me a cup of tea. That man most definitely did not arrive since we did."

"What did you see when they wheeled him out?" I asked her, although I suspected he'd been quite covered up and hidden from view by the beardy-sounding paramedic and his colleague.

"Nothing much. He was covered over with a blanket thing, but when young Doofus got in the way, it slipped for a moment. I got a quick glimpse of his face, and although you couldn't tell much from that angle, and the paramedic jumped in pretty smartish to cover him up, there was an awful lot of blood on his shirt for someone who'd been bashed on the head, but perhaps he'd been lying in it."

"Who did your hair?"

"Bobby-Jo washed. Claude cut. Bobby-Jo coloured. She's been flitting between me and Maud. She'll be back to wash it again soon, she said."

I reached out my hand and patted around until I found my friend's head. "Oh," I said. "You are still foiled up."

"They had to cut it first. You were quicker, because you didn't have yours cut. Alice had you all wrapped up and foiled like a turkey before Claude had finished with me. I'm a good half hour or so behind you, at least." She lowered her voice again and I felt her warm breath on my cheek as she whispered, "Is Maud all right? She seems awfully flustered."

"Everyone is flustered," I answered. "Alice was quite a-tremble, earlier. She had pulled herself together for a while, but I think it just hit her all over again. Maud is worried because Alice is worried. It's not every day you find a dead man in your workplace, after all. Or anywhere, come to think of it. I wouldn't be surprised if it's the first corpse the poor girl has ever seen. And that poor little Lily. I'm awfully glad they let her go home. What a frightful shock."

"And our Claude is flapping like a fish on a hook, trying to appear calm for everyone else, the poor man. It will be terrible for business. What a mess."

"Might not. People do love a bit of drama. He might get a sudden rush of new, nosey clients. You never know. What's Flora been up to all afternoon? Can you see the desk from there?"

"Hang on, let me look." Phyllis let go of my arms and stepped away, so I supposed she must be craning her neck to look around the mirror.

"Still at the desk. She's mostly been flicking through magazines, filing her nails, and trying to answer the phone before Doofus snatches it out of her hand. She's been up and down to the door a few times, too."

"Nothing I didn't know. Anything else? Does she seem calm? Is *anyone* looking at all *shifty*?"

"Flora's as cool as an icy pavement in December. The only time I saw her get at all animated was when she was chatting to you. I caught snippets, of course. Seems our corpse was not much liked by anyone. He wasn't a nice man. But *I* could have told you that. Alice isn't the first girl he'd cheated on and she won't be the—oh! Whoops a daisy. Yes she will."

"Silver linings, hmm," I said, because at least that was true.

From behind Phyllis, there was the soft *thnk* of a book being closed, and Annabel chipped in. "You're right. He wasn't exactly popular around here, I can tell you. Tried it on with a friend of mine, so he did. Didn't want to take no. She threatened him with the cops and had a word with the barman. Put a stop to it, but all the same ..." A chair scraped across the floor, and the light darkened then brightened fractionally. "Excuse me, P.C. Finbury, but is it all right if I pop to the loo?"

He grudgingly gave her permission, and then, God bless the woman, she managed to engage him in conversation for several minutes, too, and by the sound of their voices, they'd drifted over towards the reception desk, which gave Phyl and me a little breathing space to confer. I suspect by then Finbury was just as bored as the rest of us and longing for another cigarette break, which gave me another idea.

"Phyl, where are Claude and Gordon and Bobby-Jo right now?"

"They went over to sit in the waiting area for a bit. None of them have anything pressing to do here, until my hair needs to come out. Everyone else is finished. Flora had to turn away the rest of the day's clients. Claude's face looked a picture of sorrow; worse even than when he realised he had a dead man in his cupboard. He looked quite cross about *that*. There's nothing more to sweep or wash or tidy, and none of them are allowed to get into the cupboard, so it's all just a waiting game now, until they arrest someone and let the rest of us go home."

"When Bobby-Jo comes back, ask her to see if any of them can lure Doofus outside for a smoke? Then we can all talk more freely."

"Okey dokey, will try."

"Meanwhile, I'm going to go back to my seat to sit quietly and think about it for a while, because I really think it has to be one of the salon staff, and I don't want to believe it of any of them. Let me quickly tell you what I already know." I knew I hadn't much time, so I filled her in on what Alice said was in the cupboard, and how none of those items seemed very suitable as a murder weapon, what with being either too big and bulky like the not-Henry vacuum cleaner, or too soft like the piles of towels, or too small or too fragrant. "What we really need to do, Phyllis," I said to her in the quietest whisper I could manage, "is establish that the method really was a blow to the head, because maybe we're all barking up the wrong tree and he'd been suffocated or poisoned."

"Not likely, with all that blood," Phyllis reminded me, and she had a point there.

"Stabbed, then?"

"Ooh, could be. Haven't the police said anything about that? You'd think it would be the kind of thing they'd have said. Or the paramedics." Phyllis sounded quite animated by it all, as much as one can when one is whispering, but then she always did like a good gory murder mystery. Her bookshelves used to be lined with those awful blood-thirsty thrillers, right up until she retired and turned to gentle romance instead, much to her Frederick's relief. He liked to have a little joke with us about how worried he was she would bludgeon him to death in bed one night, and how he much preferred the idea of her re-enacting a steamy romance, and then he'd tell Phyllis she was blushing the colour of a beetroot and she'd put my hand to her cheek so I could feel the heat.

"I haven't heard them say anything. Alice was the one who said he'd been bashed, and she was in quite a state so might not really have taken it all in accurately, which you have to make allowances for as it must have all been a terrible shock."

The thoughts of the blood reminded me of something Phyllis had told me pertaining to Maud, and I had to think quickly about how to find out what that was all about. "Now," I said quite loudly to ensure Finbury knew why I was aiding and abetting Phyllis in breaking the rules about staying at her seat, "since Alice is having a little cry, perhaps you could just walk me to my seat in order that I don't create any further chaos by toppling into the Christmas tree or any such palaver."

Obligingly, she took my arm, and we were suddenly just two elderly ladies taking a leisurely stroll, albeit locked inside a rather steamy hair salon with a killer at large.

I made my steps deliberately slow and shuffling as we ambled towards my seat, and Phyl immediately guessed something was afoot as she slowed her gait to match mine without complaint or question, and I whispered under my breath for her to bend her head closer.

Her breath was warm on my cheek, and her foil-wrapped hair scraped against my skin. I didn't waste the precious time we had out of Maud's and Alice's earshot so hastily whispered instructions telling Phyllis to ask Maud if the coffee stain had come out, being sure to use those exact words in the hopes of wrong-footing her, even though we couldn't be sure whether it was coffee she had spilled. "Try to get a good look at it, if you can. See if there's any trace? Report back to me as soon as you are able."

Phyllis gave a little gasp and I could tell she was excited about this little investigative mission with which she had been tasked.

"It's thrilling, isn't it?" she whispered, and I nudged her gently with my elbow to remind her that someone was dead and someone amongst us must be the killer, but I'm sure she understood that despite the horror of it all, I couldn't help but agree with her. It was terribly thrilling.

Once Phyllis had helped me tap my way back to my seat, I closed my eyes for what might look to Doofus to be forty winks, which would keep him out of my hair, but really I was piecing together the parts in my mind and thinking a stabbing would be altogether more probable on several counts.

Count One: Nothing Alice had described seemed entirely practical for hitting someone over the head, especially if one's intention was to kill someone. Although, if the intent was merely to defend or stun, a hefty bottle of shampoo may suffice.

Whilst I had been immediately dismissive of the idea, it was, of course, entirely possible that the killer had not intended to kill. *Had* someone bashed Robert J. Robertson in defence? Alice and Flora and now Annabel had all suggested he was *entirely* the kind of person one may need to fight off, so it could be perfectly plausible someone had tried just that, and it had gone terribly wrong.

But if that were so, why not admit the incident?

Perhaps, by the time one realises one has killed someone, one is less inclined to admit they resorted to an act of such violence, however justified it may have seemed in the moment.

I could imagine the interrogation: "Tell me, Mrs Smith, was it absolutely necessary to clobber the man with such force that you split open his skull?" I shuddered, and brushed the thought away.

And even if that were so, it did little to explain what the man was doing in the cupboard in the first place, and why no one knew he was there.

With these thoughts and mysteries churning in my mind, I longed above all for a notepad and pencil. One of the things I have found most impractical about losing my eyesight is the inability to write things down. It is most frustrating when one is attempting to solve a puzzle, but unable to take notes which one can study, doodle upon, rearrange, and annotate. But I have, once again, allowed myself to digress.

Count Two: Among the suspects, most are not substantially built. Claude is slim and wiry although he is at least a foot taller than me, I should think, these days. He has thin, bony hands with delicate fingers that run gently through one's hair in a most pleasing manner. He treads softly, and can be terribly amusing at times, especially when he gets excited.

Gordon is taller and is that type of man who goes to the gym quite frequently, so he would be one who could brandish a fire extinguisher and smash it on a man's head, I suppose, but Claude is terribly fond of him and I always thought Claude to be a good judge of character, although I suppose you can't really be certain of anybody, these days. I sense him towering above me when he attends to my hair—Gordon, that is, so he must be a good six inches taller than Claude at the very least—although I usually get shared between Claude and Alice, for continuity or whatnot, so I don't often get to chat to Gordon. He smells of citrus and spice, which you might think would remind one of a Christmas cake mixture, but it's not like that at all. Gordon is a quieter, more serious kind of man in comparison to bubbly Claude so I expect there is some truth in opposites attracting. Take Dennis and me, for instance. We are quite dissimilar, despite having been married since 1972.

Alice always was a petite little thing; barely taller than me, although I do appear to have shrunk in the wash over the years. Annabel, I cannot picture with any accuracy, but her voice is small and soft, and I find softly-spoken women are often soft-footed and delicate to match, but it is of no consequence, as she is not a likely suspect at all, given her late arrival on the scene. Josephine is sturdy and statuesque, at about five-seven, but she has suffered with her back for as long as I can recall, and even if she had arrived in the salon at such an hour as to secretly meet Robert J. Robertson, lure him into the cupboard through a locked front door, and decide that was the most suitable place to kill him, I doubt she could wield a shampoo bottle with any degree of strength.

Maud, Phyllis and I are ladies of a certain age, by which time of life the use of upper arm strength is largely reserved for baking, crochet, knitting, or embroidery. All those, of course, are pleasures of which I am now deprived, barring those days when someone is kind enough to make time to assist me in the kitchen. I do enjoy some terribly pleasant afternoons with my granddaughter, who is quite the baker. Nonetheless, and regardless of the quality of one's eyesight, any woman of such age and disposition seems unlikely to possess sufficient ability to hoist anything heavier than a hairbrush to a height worthy to plummet onto a man's head with force enough to topple him, don't you agree? And I cannot imagine he was killed with a hairbrush.

Flora is usually seated behind the desk when I visit the salon and one cannot gain an accurate idea of a person's height while they are seated, especially when one has restricted vision. On that particular Thursday, for a short time, our situations were reversed, with I the seated, and she towering over me as she was dispatched to keep me company. She only remained standing for the briefest moment, and in that time, her words fell in the air far above my ears, until she sank herself into Alice's seat and I could hear her better. I cursed myself inwardly at my lack of foresight. I needed to engineer a conversation in which we would both stand, although from the sound of her shoes, she wears an impractically tall heel. Even in my youth, I found it impossible to balance in anything taller than a neat kitten heel, so I don't know how she manages without wobbling, but of course, many girls do.

Bobby-Jo is of average height, and she certainly used to have a very trim figure. Like Gordon, she is fond of the gym, as I often hear the two of them discussing their activities, and asking one another if they are 'working out' after work, although in my day that meant solving a mathematical challenge. Bobby-Jo always was more the sporty type than the academic type, although I do recall her saying she might do one of those Open University courses but I can't tell you whether she followed it through. She might be strong enough to wield a hefty weapon, but unless Robert J. Robertson was a very short man, I cannot imagine she would have got it high enough. There is not room in that cupboard to swing a weapon sideways, in the manner of one swinging a baseball bat, and had one attempted such a thing, I have little doubt they would have swept several objects from the shelves in their efforts. As I had tapped my cane about the doorway, whilst searching for the source of the smell, I did not encounter any fallen objects, although I do concede there may have been some further into the cupboard, beyond the scope of my cane. Would someone have tidied up after themselves? I can't imagine so.

Besides, I had already ascertained that Bobby-Jo attended the nativity play in the primary school earlier that day, and even the most athletic type of person could not kill a man at that distance, even if they were an Olympian shot-putter or javelin thrower. Flora had mentioned something about Bobby-Jo leaving early and I supposed she must have meant early to get off to her son's play, given the context of the information. She had clearly told me Bobby-Jo *had* left early, and not that she was *going to* leave early. None of us, it seemed apparent by then, would be doing *that*.

That only leaves little Lily, who, I believe, is short and chubby and still hoping to grow into herself, according to the passing comments I have picked up over the course of the afternoon. I imagine her as a round-faced, dumpy little thing, although I am sure she is quite pretty in her own way and she always seems terribly sweet. Nonetheless, I needed to establish how tall the dead man was. A question for Alice.

But, altogether, I was beginning to think it unlikely that the man had, indeed, had his head bashed in, given the evidence. Or lack thereof.

Count Three: Stabbing is the kind of thing anyone can do, given a suitable implement. A quick thrust into a soft belly, or an uppercut into a chest or neck, perhaps. A stab in the back with a carving knife, or a slash into a wrist or femur. I imagine it would be an easy enough thing to hit an artery, whether by accident or design. The height of one's victim does not come into the matter, I shouldn't think. Phyllis would know. Her thriller novels would be packed with this kind of information. Positively *oozing* with details. Oozing like blood from a knife wound. Oozing onto a man's shirtfront, quite unlike a wound sustained to the back of one's head, wouldn't you think?

A shiver tickled the back of my neck and the temperature in the room dropped by several degrees. Sure enough, the call of thanks from a plethora of voices and a whoosh of chilly

December air around my ankles heralded the arrival of the sandwiches, and not a moment too soon. My stomach gave a loud grumble of recognition and Flora said, "Oh, plates too, well done," to whoever had delivered the food, and then the door was shut once more, and the key turned again on our temporary prison.

Chapter Eleven

Dear Alice fetched me a ham sandwich and a cheese sandwich on a floppy paper plate, which she set carefully onto my lap.

"Would you like crisps, too?" she asked, which was thoughtful.

I don't often have crisps these days, so it felt like a bit of a treat, which tickled me, considering the circumstances. Anyway, she fetched me a packet of ready-salted, because I didn't want to have cheese-and-onion breath when I still had no idea how long we might be incarcerated in the salon, and I do find salt-and-vinegar a little ... well, a little vinegary, which I suppose one would expect from that flavour, so I can't complain.

She opened the pack with a rustle and a pop, but rather than hand them to me she suggested she rearrange me a little so I may avail of the shelf as a kind of table, and would that make it easier for me?

"It would," I said, so she took up my paper plate again and set it down onto the shelf, and by the rustling of the crisp packet I could tell she'd put those down too. "Now hold tight to the arms, Mrs Smith, and I'll push you in."

I chuckled. "Fasten your seat belt and enjoy the ride," I said, affecting the manner of a fair ride assistant, and Alice gave me a gentle shove and it was more exciting than one might think. "Ooh," I said, with another little giggle, "we could go all around the salon, after our snack, if we are still in need of something to occupy ourselves."

Alice laughed, and so did Josephine and Phyllis, so the atmosphere had been considerably lightened by the arrival of sustenance.

While Alice and Phyllis and Josephine and I appeared to be enjoying our sandwiches, D.S. Nasir asked Maud what she could get for her, and said they would eat theirs together in the staff room, along with D.I. Nelson, if Maud was okay with that. Really, what could she say? I am sure she would have preferred not to, but one can't argue with the police, unless it's Dougal Rufus, that is, so Maud went with the Detective Sergeant as meekly as a sheep following its flock, and said she'd like two ham sandwiches and a packet of cheese-and-onion please.

For a while after Maud went off with the two senior police officers, the salon was filled with the steady near-silence of several people trying to eat their sandwiches as quietly as possible. Of course, the efforts at eating with any level of decorum went out of the window as soon as we started on the crisps, and that made everyone laugh and loosen up a bit.

With the cold December air outside the salon, and the number of people inside, all of us breathing and eating, the air had become quite steamed-up and the whole salon had that vibe of a cosy gathering-space on a dark winter's night. I'm sure if we had only been allowed to converse freely and mingle, the atmosphere would have been quite festive.

"Phyl," I called hopefully towards the mirror in front of me. "Would you please tell me if the salon has been adorned with Christmas decorations? I noticed a distinct whiff of fresh pine as we entered the salon, so I presume there might be a tree?"

She heard me well enough, and said, yes, there was a most impressive tree in the window, and then Annabel added that the one at reception was almost as big and took up half the counter, and someone else laughed and agreed yes, wasn't it, and suddenly everyone began chipping in to describe not only the festive look of the salon—artistically decked out in purple and gold, apparently, so I had to adjust my mental image of that, but it does show that one doesn't always have to follow the traditional red and green colour scheme one tends to equate with Christmas—but also the lights on the high street. The council kept the lights up all year, which I suppose is more convenient than sending men up in one of those nifty cherry-picker contraptions, but it was a long time since I'd been able to see them with any real clarity and it was very pleasant indeed to have them described to me through so many fresh eyes.

Dougal Rufus must have decided it was harmless enough and didn't prevent this topic of conversation, and I must say it made me feel quite Christmassy and that really, Flora should have asked the hotel to send some mince pies and brandy with the sandwiches. I wondered if it was worth asking but decided not to bother, as I was still optimistic we'd be released quite soon.

Alice was still having moments of teary sniffles in between putting a brave face on the matter, and I made a mental note to suggest to the nice Detective Sergeant, or perhaps the Detective Inspector chap, that she may be in shock after discovering the corpse, and maybe should be allowed to leave, although I supposed they still hoped to make an arrest before allowing us out. I tried my best to reassure her, but when one can't be entirely certain who amongst us had killed the man in cold blood, I don't imagine she was altogether comforted by my platitudes. I didn't entirely believe them myself. I must say I was surprised Maud hadn't tried to be a bit more supportive, as I know I would do anything for my grandchildren, but Maud is a stickler for rules, so maybe she didn't like to get up. I wondered how she was getting on in the interview room, and hoped that whatever she said matched Alice's side of things, or that would get a bit sticky.

Claude had calmed down a bit by now, possibly because it was after five and the salon hadn't needed to turn away any more customers for the last half hour or so and the telephone had stopped ringing so he had one less thing to worry about. Well, two things, to be precise. I do prefer to be precise, but I do get a bit muddled on occasion and you'll have to make allowances for that, at seventy-four, I'm afraid. I did hear him say a few times that he'd have to get someone in to clear up the mess in the cupboard because he certainly wasn't going to ask any of his team to do it, which was very sensitive of him and showed a great deal of compassion.

"Alice," I whispered, in between mouthfuls of my ham sandwich. "I'm sorry to ask this, but could you tell me, was there an awful lot of blood?"

"Mrs Smith! You've put me right off my sandwich! Eugh."
The shelf rattled just a fraction and I think she must have set
her plate down, but a moment later she crunched a mouthful
of crisps, so she'd obviously got over it fast enough.

"There was, a bit," she said, through a mouthful. "All over
his shirt."

Aha, I thought. "How did you know it was Mr Robertson?"
I asked, as I was still wondering how she'd identified him so
quickly, given the shock.

"Well I knew his face, of course. You don't forget someone's
face you've only just broken up from, however much you want
to." She shuddered again—I heard it in the rustle of the crisp
packet, but she rummaged in the packet and started crunching
again so she couldn't have been all that perturbed by it. Or
perhaps she was just hungry, as I'm sure she would have been
by then.

"So was he lying on his back, or his front?"

"He was looking right up at me!" Her voice rose from its
whisper and somewhere behind me Finbury's shoes squeaked
on the tiles.

"Everything all right here ladies?" His voice dripped with
insincerity and I had an overwhelming urge to bash him with
my cane, but luckily for him, I was only holding a half-eaten
ham sandwich instead, and that would certainly be no use at
all as a weapon.

"We were just chatting about the Christmas lights," I said as
sweetly as I could muster.

"Oh?" He was quite disbelieving in his tone and I had to
give him some credit for seeing through my lie, but I wasn't a
teacher for forty years for nothing. "And which of the lights

was *looking right up at you*?" he said, and I have learned, since my eyesight diminished, that one can insert a glare into one's voice, so I had no doubt he was glaring at Alice as he asked that, and to be perfectly fair, he did have a valid point.

Alice is no wallflower, and even in school she was quick-witted and good at English, so I wasn't overly surprised when she said, "Haven't you seen that freaky Santa light display? The one near the big tree by the bandstand? Follows you round with his eyes, he does. And the reindeer, too," she added for good measure.

A-plus, Alice, I thought. *A-plus for that excellent improvisation.*

"Hmph," Finbury huffed, and his shoe gave such a high-pitched squeal I bet he had spun around on the ball of his foot to stomp away. "I'll be listening to you," he warned in a low growl as he squeaked off towards the window.

"Well done, Alice," I whispered, as quietly as I could, while crumpling my crisp packet as loudly as I could. "Was there blood all around his head, or only on his shirt?"

She didn't answer straight away so I stopped crinkling the crisp packet while I gave her time to visualise the unpleasant scene in her mind.

After a moment of silence, she gave her crisp packet a little rustle, and said, "I guess not, really. I don't really want to think about it." Rustle, rustle, rustle. She was cottoning on fast.

"I know," I said, "but it might be important."

Rustle, rustle, rustle.

"More on the front of his shirt, I'd say, than round his head."

"What was he wearing?"

She munched on a sandwich while she thought about it, so I had another bite of mine, too.

"A light-grey polo shirt, under a grey hoody. That's the company uniform. The type that zips all the way, but unzipped. There's a little truck logo embroidered on the pocket—the shirt and the hoody." She swallowed another bite of her sandwich. "Jeans. Nike trainers. He always wore those."

"Was he a tall man?"

Munch. Munch. Swallow.

"Taller than me. Not quite as tall as Gord." Rustle. Crumple. "About Claude's height, I should say. Give or take."

"Were his feet nearest the door, or his head?" I tried to recapture the shape I'd felt with my cane, but as I hadn't expected it to be a man's body, and had imagined it to be a heap of towels, I really didn't want to consider which parts of his anatomy I might have inadvertently prodded as I'd tapped my cane further into the cupboard and onto the dark shape on the floor. That was *not* an image I wished to carry in my mind.

"Feet," she whispered under a fresh wave of rustling. "Like he'd just keeled over backward and hit his head on the shelves on his way down."

Was it possible that he had simply slipped and fallen, then, and all this confounded police interrogation was a complete waste of time? I had to suppose they'd seen something to raise their suspicions and lead them to think otherwise.

"Alice, I want you to think very carefully. Did you notice anything else on the floor? Anything at all that seemed out of place?"

"Okay, you two, that's enough!" Finbury squeaked across the room at a great speed and the single, feeble thud as he reached us could very well have been the petulant stamp of his foot, or his over-inflated ego bursting like a wet soap bubble. "Alice Devine, I am going to have to insist you go and sit over there, if you can't manage to stop your gossiping." He sounded exactly like a small child might sound if they were playing dress-up and had chosen to wear the plastic policeman's helmet with too-tight elastic under the chin.

"All right, all right, keep your hair on, Dougal," Alice retorted, as if the two of them were back in school and he had no authority over her whatsoever, but she didn't say anymore after that, and I could hear the soft sounds of her chewing her sandwich, punctuated by the occasional crunch of crisps.

Taking her cue, I patted around on the glass shelf until I found my cheese sandwich, leaned back against the soft padding of the chair, and stored the information about Robert J. Robertson's dead body with the other snippets of information I'd gleaned so far, wondering who I could manage to talk to next.

Chapter Twelve

In the relatively quiet minutes that followed, whilst Alice and I chewed our sandwiches and didn't speak to one another for fear of raising the wrath of Finbury, fragments of other conversations fluttered around my ears.

Gordon, from over towards the reception desk—probably sitting on the L-shaped bench, I shouldn't wonder—was fretting about Pumpkin, in case they weren't home to let her out to do her business. Pumpkin is Claude's and Gordon's little poodle. She is, they have told me on countless occasions, one of those darling little apricot-coloured toy poodles that remind me of ballerinas in the way they walk around on tip-toe. They hadn't wanted to call her Apricot as it really didn't suit her, somehow, so after much deliberation they'd agreed on Pumpkin, and whenever I popped into the salon, they would tell me about something she had done and I am quite certain a first-time mother with a new-born child would struggle to find such exuberant stories to tell about their flesh and blood as Claude and Gordon tell about their little poodle.

Nevertheless, it was a sobering thought that the poor creature had been alone all day and might be desperate to relieve herself and worrying that her masters had vanished from her life. I was deeply reassured that Amity was suffering no such fate, and that Dennis and she would most likely be quite happily relaxing in the lounge with a cup of tea, because even Dennis can manage to make a cup of tea, and it was about the time for one. When Amity is off-duty, she is permitted to snooze on the sofa if she so wishes, and I had no doubt that would be exactly what she would be doing in my absence. It is probably a blessing that I can no longer see the amount of dog-hair she undoubtably sheds onto the upholstery.

More snippets of inconsequential conversation ebbed and flowed, largely uninterrupted now by Finbury, who was chewing very loudly over by the window although I am not entirely sure that he was allowed to eat on the job and I wondered if he would be reprimanded by his seniors were they to catch him in the act, but they'd allowed him to take cigarette breaks, so perhaps the force has become more lenient about things like that now. Or perhaps it was a special technique taught in Police Training, designed to lull suspects into thinking he is just an ordinary person to whom they might reveal more than they otherwise might.

After another interminable number of minutes had passed, I caught a far more interesting snatch of information and I immediately paused in my own steady chewing and pricked up my ears.

"Why did you come back? At lunchtime, I mean?" It was Gordon's voice, still, and I strained my ears to establish to whom he had directed the question. I didn't think he'd said it loudly enough to be asking Alice, who I believed was still beside me, although she had fallen into a long silence ever since she had finished her crisps and set the empty packet down on the shelf.

"I'd forgotten to bring my card with me," Flora said evenly. "I'd taken it out of my purse earlier, to pay for something, and ran out for lunch without remembering to pick it up again."

"You were here a good few minutes," Gordon said, with a hint of accusation.

"I couldn't find it, at first. It was on the floor. Took me a minute." There was a beat of silence, then she asked, "How do you know I came back?" If Gordon's voice had been mildly accusing, Flora's was positively laced with suspicion. "Were you here?" she hissed, and I was sure Finbury must have heard her, but he didn't move so maybe he was too engrossed in his sandwich, or picking crumbs out of his teeth.

"Saw you from the pub window while I was watching for Claude and wondering where he'd got to."

"Yes, Claude was still there. I told the police all about it, anyway," Flora said. "But if you were watching from the pub, you'd have seen that we left together as soon as I found my card, and anyway, didn't you see anything more useful? Like Sleazeball Robertson arriving with the delivery, for instance?"

Claude agreed with Flora, and said he'd been about to leave when she flew in, so he'd made sure she found her card in case she couldn't and he needed to lend her a tenner from the till, and Flora said that was true, so they backed each other up quite well, I thought, although it didn't give Claude much of an alibi for the ten minutes or so that he'd been alone in the salon, and who's to say whether Robert J. had already been bleeding out in the cupboard while Claude nonchalantly helped Flora find her missing bank card?

Gordon gave a little "hmph" at that, and said he'd seen Alice and Maud come in, too, just before he left the pub after finishing his lunch, but rather than expand on that, he swung the conversation back around to the little dog left at home fretting about his masters.

"But Gord," Claude said, in his reassuring tones, "you nipped home to let her out, didn't you? At lunchtime? She'll be fine. We wouldn't usually be home yet, even on an ordinary day. Silly." I imagined him dropping a comforting hand on Gordon's arm, as Gordon replied in a slightly calmer voice to say Claude was quite right, of course.

I needed to find out whether Gordon had popped home to the dog when he first left for his lunch break, which I remembered he'd said he'd taken a little early as he was finished with his client, or if he had popped home after he and Claude had finished their lunch, while Claude had gone to the newsagent. Or if indeed he had not gone home at all and was worrying about poor Pumpkin because he had *not* gone home at lunchtime to let her out but had instead nipped back into the salon to biff that Robertson chap about the head and kill him. I wondered, too, about Flora's pertinent comment. If Gordon had been watching the salon from the pub window, had he, in fact, seen Robertson approach the salon, and if so, why had he not said as much?

"Alice," I whispered, as softly as I could manage. "Shall we take another little trip to the lavatory?" She gave my arm a tiny squeeze, which I took as assent, so I got myself to my feet and took up my cane. "Oh, Dougal," I called, in my sweet old-lady voice, "Alice is just going to help me to the lavatories to wash my hands after those delicious sandwiches. We won't be a minute." Without waiting for his objections, Alice tucked her hand into my elbow, and we scurried off to the ladies' as fast as an almost-blind seventy-four-year-old can scurry.

As the door swung closed behind us, Alice immediately turned on the tap and I took advantage of the situation to give my hands a little rinse, but also to ask her what time Gordon and Claude had returned after their lunch.

"Oh, I don't know exactly," she said, but then she gave the matter a little more thought and added that she thought Gordon had got back a few minutes ahead of Claude, and hadn't I arrived at around about the same time as both of them, so that corroborated Gordon's story quite nicely but didn't help me to work out who might have killed Robertson, or even throw any more light on *when* he may have been killed.

"Is it always Gordon who pops home to Pumpkin at lunchtimes?" I asked her next, as I thought maybe if I could establish their regular routines, it may help me to notice a discrepancy.

"Oh, no, I wouldn't say so. It might be either of them. I've even run in for them once or twice, if they've both been very busy. Flora or Bobby too, now and then. They do try to get to her themselves, most days. They often both go home for lunch anyway. Easy when it's so close."

Gordon and Claude share a very nice flat a little further along the high street, stretching over the solicitor's office *and* the florist. It's a terribly luxurious flat, by all accounts, and quite spacious, with a view over the park. Claude has described it to me in great detail over the years and his latest home improvement was to redo the living room in a very expensive wallpaper. I told him I simply couldn't imagine a wallpaper could cost that much, unless it were a hand-painted, centuries-old design from an ancient imperial palace or suchlike, and Claude had laughed and said he wouldn't be surprised if it was even nicer than that, and they were very pleased with it. It's such a shame they can't live right over the top of the salon, I always think, but the rooms above the salon have been taken by a podiatrist for as long as I can remember and are nowhere near as large. I do question the logic of expecting anyone with foot problems to get themselves up those stairs, and it smells most obnoxiously of foot odour and can't possibly be as nice as Claude's swanky flat overlooking the park.

"But Gordon went to her today?"

"That's what they said. Gord said he'd pop home to her because he had a longer lunchbreak."

"And did he actually go, do you know? And at what time?"

"No idea." Alice turned me to the hand drier and pressed the button, resulting in a welcome rush of warm air and whoosh of noise.

"Remind me again what time you and your Gran returned to the salon? And whether anyone else was here when you returned," I said, as I waved my hands back and forth under the blast.

"We came back at about twelve-forty-five, I'd guess. We'd been to the café for lunch, and it was really busy, so we had to give up the table as soon as we were done eating. We didn't hang around. We were going to stroll back slowly, do some window-shopping on the way, you know? But then Gran realised she needed a wee and we were already away from the café by then, and she didn't want to go back. That's why we came back here so early. Daft old bat." She gave one of those little half-chuckles as she said that so I don't think she really meant it about Maud being a daft old bat, although she can be a bit difficult at times if you ask me.

That reminded me about the other thing I needed to ask Alice, so I bashed the button to start the drier off again and said, "Alice, Phyllis said she thought you seemed upset when we first arrived. Was there anything troubling you?"

She didn't say anything for a moment and then she gave a little snort and said in quite a sharp tone that finding a dead man on the floor would upset anyone wouldn't it, and I agreed and then said I meant before that, though, when we first arrived in the salon after lunch and she was making her grandmother a nice cup of tea.

"Phyllis said when you brought the tea to Maud, you ..." I grasped around for a balance of words that would not sound as if I were prying, even though prying was exactly my intent at this juncture. "Well, dear, what I mean is, are you *all right*? Aside from this bother with Robertson, that is?"

She was quiet again for a moment and then gave a little huffy sigh and a sniff and said very quietly, "It was nothing," so I was none the wiser.

I couldn't ask her anything more about it because a loud rapping on the door made me jump a little, and I think Alice did too because she made a teeny little squealing noise like my daughter's guinea pig used to when it wanted to get out of its cage. A long time ago, of course. She is all grown up with children of her own and they don't have a guinea pig but do have two short-haired cats, which are altogether easier to look after if you ask me.

Finbury's bad-tempered voice yelled through the door that he was sure we must have washed our hands by now and out we come or he'd have to open the door and check we weren't conspiring, so we had to leave the ladies' and return to our seats.

By that time, I was beginning to suspect something didn't quite add up and someone had to be lying, and whoever it was who was lying was quite likely to be the killer, too, I should think, and what I really needed to do was speak to Claude or Gordon again to get to the bottom of things, and I needed to find a Finbury-proof way to engineer it.

For a fleeting moment, and not for the first time that afternoon, I longed to feel Amity resting her head on my knee, or nudging me gently with her nose. If she were here, I thought, I could have feigned needing to take her outside to do her business, although of course she is trained well enough to not need to do any such thing in the space of four hours in a hair salon, but I doubt Finbury would have known about that, and I could have requested Claude accompany me out to the tiny patch of scrubby courtyard that backs onto the row of properties along the high street that one can access through a narrow side alley if one has hold of the right person's arm to guide them. There are, before you ask, no windows or back entryways into the salon from this rear outside space, although goodness only knows why, so there is no possibility of any assailant or delivery man entering Claude's Curls from any point other than via its doorway on the High Street.

Without Amity's presence to provide an excuse to vacate the salon, I needed to rack my little grey cells for another idea, as that wonderful Poirot would say, but before I could come up with any such plan, Phyllis, bless her, seemed to have read my mind, or at least have remembered to fulfil my instructions, because not a minute after I was returned to my seat by Alice, I heard Phyllis whispering something I didn't catch. Nor, at first, did I know to whom she directed her whisper.

"Gotcha," a voice whispered back, and it must have been Bobby-Jo because a few seconds later, she said quite loudly that she was dying, *just dying* for a cigarette, and would it really hurt for the smokers to pop outside for a breath of fresh air. I never did quite understand how smokers referred to their cigarette indulgence as 'fresh air' but I was more than happy to overlook this incongruity if it got Dougal Finbury out of the salon for a minute or two.

Annabel chimed up then, adding her voice to Bobby-Jo's, and then Finbury said he supposed if they left the salon door open and he stood in the doorway he could watch the two smokers and the inside of the salon at the same time. I knew full well what he really meant was that he needed a cigarette too, because even as a spotty fifteen-year-old, he was forever nipping off behind the gym where the smokers thought the teachers couldn't find them. When one is a teacher for forty years, one learns which battles to fight, and that, I can tell you, was not one of them. We all knew the smokers. If the reek of tobacco on their uniforms and in their hair didn't give them away, the excessive gum-chewing, the yellowed fingers, and the pallid expressions were certain pointers. It was simply that we had concluded long ago that it was easier to let them gather behind the gymnasium out of sight from the public, than fend off complaints about teenage delinquents smoking in the street or the park or wherever they chose to loiter in those days, with their school ties stuffed in their blazer pockets and their shirts untucked.

Some habits never change, and although I was quite certain that now, as then, it was frowned upon to smoke whilst in uniform, I bit back the urge to reprimand him as I really did want him to step outside and allow me a moment with Claude or Gordon.

To my surprise, Gordon, over by the reception desk somewhere, said quite loudly that he'd kill for a fag too, which made some people laugh, although I must say in my day that word referred only to a cigarette and had none of that double meaning, and it didn't occur to me for a minute that Gordon meant it in any other manner, but when the ripple of laughter ran around the salon it got me thinking about whether there *might* in fact be a double meaning in Gordon's words, and would he kill for Claude if it came to it? I believe it's a terribly insulting word used in certain circumstances, but for Gordon and Claude, of course, if that was how they chose to refer to themselves, well that was their prerogative, I should think, wouldn't you? Everyone had said that Claude was terribly annoyed with Robert J. Robertson, and one really never can be quite certain to what lengths one may go for someone they love, so it was certainly *possible* that Gordon had taken it upon himself to relieve dear Claude of the unpleasantness that was Robert J. Robertson, by all accounts.

Nonetheless, my surprise was not over Gordon's choice of words. The thought that had struck me with immediate ferocity was that, to the best of my knowledge, he didn't smoke. I have never smelled any hint of tobacco about his person. Indeed, he always smells frightfully clean and fresh, along with that spicy, citrussy aftershave he uses. I said as much to Alice, and she chuckled a little and said he doesn't, but she guessed he just wanted an excuse to get out of the salon and then I had a vision of him running off down the high street with Finbury dashing after him. If there is one thing I will say about Dougal Rufus, it's that he was quite a decent runner, in his day. I expect he kept that up at Police Training College too, as I suppose one has to be fit, to be a police constable, although they all sit at desks most of the time these days rather than plodding about on the beat so perhaps police officers have become fatter, nowadays.

Anyway, Bobby-Jo and Annabel and Gordon must have huddled in the doorway with Finbury straddling the threshold and I don't expect Claude was very happy about the image that was giving his business, but perhaps by then he didn't care very much as we were all quite fed up with it all by that time, even though it was still only about quarter past five and not even very late.

The draught that blew in from the high street was chilly but woke me up a bit, and a hum of Christmas-shopper chatter wafted in with the breeze, which reminded us of the world going on quite normally outside the salon, which was a bit strange but quite refreshing. I was glad of the re-invigorating draught and noise, to be perfectly frank, as I had been in danger of nodding off. Instead, I grabbed the chance, as they say, and asked Alice to beckon Claude over as quick as she could without Finbury noticing, and sure enough, he came at once and sank into Alice's chair with a long sigh.

He reached to pat my knee just as I groped about to touch his arm, and we accidentally exchanged one of those new-fangled high-five gestures and turned it into a funny little handshake like those Freemason men, so that was a light moment in the afternoon as well.

"I wasn't aware that Gordon was a smoker," I said, as an opener.

"He isn't, not really. Gave it up about six years ago."

"He's having one now, though?"

"Can't say I blame him. Tempted myself, Mrs S. Tempted myself." He paused for a moment in which neither of us said anything, then added, "Aren't you? I'd say we're all about ready to get out of here." He laughed, but it wasn't a very cheerful kind of laugh and I felt terribly sorry for him in that moment.

"What's going on now?" I asked him, as I tried to recall what it was I had wanted to find out.

"They've still got Maud in the staffroom. But it's only been ten minutes or so."

I was surprised to hear that, as it felt as if we'd been sitting here for hours, and couldn't possibly be only ten minutes since Detective Sergeant Nasir had taken Maud off to be interviewed over a paper plate of sandwiches, so it's probably true what they say about time slowing down when you most want it to speed up a bit.

"Gord's been worrying about Pumpkin," Claude said. "He didn't let her out at lunchtime." There was a note of worry in his voice, and I couldn't be sure whether it was worry about the little dog, or worry that Gordon had not been exactly where he'd said he'd be, and I thought for a moment about what to say to that.

"I am quite relieved that Amity doesn't like your salon very much," I said, after a moment. "I'm glad I don't have to worry about getting her home for her supper. Dennis will have fed her by now, I should think. I do hope Dennis manages to find himself something to eat, without setting fire to anything. Where did Gordon go, when he left the pub, if he didn't go home to poor Pumpkin, and is there anyone you can call to attend to her while you are confined here?" For the second time in as many minutes, I had a vision of Gordon running from Finbury, and this time, in my mind, he raced home along the shopper-strewn pavement, darting up and down the kerb and in and out of traffic, frantically unlocking the door to their stairwell, and bounding up the stairs to their lavishly-carpeted abode, in the hope he would get there before the poor poodle urinated on the rug.

"They let me call Laura. She said she'll pop up and take her for a run in the park."

Laura is the florist and I think I mentioned that Claude's flat is above the florist. Laura is very sweet and obliging so I don't suppose she minded at all about Pumpkin.

"Claude," I said, resting my fingers on his arm, "why exactly did Gordon say he was going to attend to Pumpkin if he did no such thing?" I was a little flabbergasted to think that anyone as devoted to their dog as Gordon appeared to be would compromise her comfort without a very good reason, and I needed to discern exactly what that reason had been if I was to remove Gordon from my mental list of most likely suspects.

"He told me," Claude said miserably, "that he had to go and collect my Christmas present and that he knew he would finish early today so Pumpkin could wait another hour until he could go home straight after finishing with Josephine's hair."

He paused for a fraction, then gave another heavy sigh. "The trouble is, Mrs S., I'm not actually sure if I believe him, as when I watched him from the pub window, he was walking towards the salon."

Chapter Thirteen

I asked Claude whether he had mentioned that news to the nice Detective Sergeant, and he didn't answer that but instead, he told me something else that was even worse.

"And, I'm fairly sure there was a delivery van parked just a little bit along the high street, outside the bakery, or thereabouts. It might have been Robertson's van I saw, but I can't be certain. I only glanced at it; didn't think anything of it. It was only when the copper said the van had been spotted by old Willie at twelve-ten that I wondered about it, you know?"

Old Willie has been the traffic warden in Little Wittering for at least thirty years and he is not the town's most popular resident by anyone's standards but he's a perfectly pleasant man when you get to know him. People do tend to stereotype traffic wardens, which is terribly short-sighted and not a little unkind. Willie lives a few doors along from me and Dennis, and has a cat called Martha who is very fond of Amity. Martha usually comes in for a little piece of fish on Fridays, when we have fish for supper, you see, which is how she got to know Amity. Martha wasn't quite sure at first, but Amity is trained for that sort of thing and knows how to behave around cats so it wasn't a problem for long.

"Of course, even if it was Robertson's van, he'd usually have a few deliveries to do on the High Street, so there's still no way of knowing what time he called to the salon or who let him in ..." Claude's voice tailed off but I could tell he was awfully worried by this information and I could see why he might want to keep it to himself about Gordon not being in the right place at the right time, or even quite possibly being in the wrong place at the right time, if you see what I mean.

"And is the van still there?" I asked. "Has it been confirmed whether it is indeed Robertson's delivery van?"

Claude said, "Mmm," which I suspected might mean it was the right van, but it might have meant he didn't know, although you'd have thought he'd have said so if that were the case.

"What did Gordon buy you?"

"He won't say. Says it will ruin the surprise, Mrs S., which is fair enough, if only ... well, you know?"

I said I did know, and I thought it might be best if I had a word with Gordon and maybe he'd tell me what the gift was and then I could reassure Claude that Gordon was telling the truth and put his mind at rest, without spoiling the Christmas surprise in any way.

"If we don't get out of here soon," Claude said with a dry laugh, "we'll miss Christmas anyway!"

I did appreciate his attempts to lighten the mood again, and forced a little chuckle in return. "Send Gordon over to me as soon as he comes back in, and I'll see if I can't find out something. Do try not to fret. I'm sure it will all be all right." Of course, I was sure of no such thing, and was only certain that for at least one of us present in the salon, things would be far from all right, and Christmas served behind bars, but I did so hope it wasn't Claude or Gordon or any of the people in the salon, although I couldn't see any possible way to conclude that it wasn't *one* of them who had killed the man.

As we were quietly contemplating the situation and each silently wondering if Gordon might have been the one to kosh Robertson and leave him to die in a pool of his own blood, the smokers came in from the cold and Maud came out of the staffroom with Detective Sergeant Nasir. Everyone was talking at once for a moment and even Finbury seemed to have given up trying to stop anyone from chattering. I only caught snippets but none of it seemed important until Finbury said the tow truck had just turned up to remove the van and maybe he should go out and supervise it if he could be spared for a few minutes, to which D.S. Nasir said yes, good idea, off you go, and then the salon door was closed again but no one bothered to lock it this time.

Not very long after that, Claude went off, and a minute later, Gordon plonked himself down in the chair beside me and sighed almost as loudly as Claude had, so it was easy to tell he was feeling terribly troubled about the whole unfortunate situation. I knew it was him before he spoke, and not only because Claude had said he'd send him over, but also from the way he dropped into the seat in a much heavier way than Alice or Claude, and the faint whiff of tobacco and the altogether more pleasant hints of that nice aftershave I told you about already.

I didn't know how much time we might have, so I was just about to go straight in with the interrogation but he got there first.

"Claude's worried I clonked that ... that ... *man* on the head and killed him," he said, quite angrily, but keeping his voice low at the same time. "Twenty-three years we've been together and now he thinks I'm a cold-blooded killer. And that I abandoned Pumpkin!" At that, he did raise his voice a little and I was interested to note he seemed significantly more distressed about neglecting his poor little dog than about the idea of having killed Robert J. Robertson.

"What did you buy Claude for Christmas?" I asked, cutting to the chase as they say.

He was silent for a moment and I picked up the faintest of plucking sounds as if he might be pulling a thread on his clothes or tapping his fingers on something soft.

"That's the trouble, Mrs Smith," he said after a short while. "It hasn't come in yet so I haven't anything to prove I was getting it, and I left poor little Pump alone for nothing and I lied to Claude about going home, and now he thinks I'm lying about where I went, too, and because of all that, he's worrying that I killed the horrible man, which I didn't, Mrs S. Really, I didn't." His voice was heavy with despair and I fumbled about until my fingers found his arm.

"I'm sure it will be all right." I gave him a little reassuring pat with my fingertips and hoped very much that I was telling the truth. "What is the gift?"

"It's a studio portrait of Pumpkin, wearing just the cutest little bowtie and she looked so adorable during the sitting, but when the frame arrived, it was damaged, so they ordered in a new one. It was supposed to arrive this morning but the delivery hadn't come yet and they said to pop back later as they were—oh!"

I guessed he must have had the same sudden idea as I had about why the delivery hadn't come, and I'm quite sure if I had been able to see him, we'd have looked at each other in that exaggerated horror-stricken way they do in the movies when the characters suddenly realise something very important.

"They said they were sure it would turn up in the next hour or so and they'd give me a call." The chair creaked faintly so it seemed as if Gordon might be readying himself to get up. "They called me at about two to say it still hadn't come and they hadn't heard from the delivery driver since he'd texted at about five to twelve to say he would be with them shortly. They said they wondered what had happened to him." Gordon spoke very fast as he told me this and I wasn't at all surprised when the next thing he said was, "I'd better go and tell the police, in case it was him."

I agreed with him, of course, because it seemed somewhat likely, don't you think, and maybe the telephone call to the photography studio was the last call he made, and if he called them at five to twelve, then he was certainly still alive at that time, and of course I couldn't be certain it was the same delivery driver but it did seem to be quite the coincidence, and detectives don't agree with coincidences. At least, not in the movies or in those audio books about police investigations.

He heaved himself from the chair with a creak and a groan, and off he went in a bit of a rush.

"Where are you going?" Finbury called, but I think Gordon might have brushed him right off, because just a moment later there was a pounding on what I presume must have been the staffroom door, as it came from that direction and I'm quite sure no one needed to be pounding on the doors to the lavatories as no one was using them at that time.

"Excuse me. Excuse me, Detectives, may I come in?"

I hadn't paid much attention to anyone else during those few minutes I was speaking with Gordon, but as Finbury was clearly still in the main body of the salon, and Gordon was calling to the other detectives through a closed door, I had to conclude that the Detective Inspector and the Detective Sergeant had retired to their makeshift interview room once more, although I couldn't tell you for certain if anyone else was in there with them as I had rather lost track of everyone at that point.

Gordon still hadn't given me any proof that he had physically walked down to the photography studios, as he could quite easily have made a telephone call to them and that would have left him time to meet Robertson in the salon and kill him in the cupboard, so I hoped the police officers were looking into that possibility and had already spoken to the photography studios, but Gordon seemed to think they hadn't, otherwise why would Claude still be so worried about it all? It was quite perplexing as I didn't want to think that Gordon could be a killer, but it did seem as if he were hiding something, don't you think?

He had risen from his chair in such a rush to share his revelation with the detectives that I had quite forgotten to ask him where exactly he had taken little Pumpkin for the photography sitting. There are two or three photographers in Little Wittering, and they are only the ones I know about—that is, the ones with proper studios in the town where anyone might pass by and call in. These days, anyone can set up a studio or a workshop and you never know what activities might be carried out from a garden shed or one of those fancy cabins that seem to have popped up all over the place in the last couple of decades. I wondered if Alice might know.

From somewhere towards the lavatories and the staffroom and the cleaning cupboard, a door opened and D.S. Nasir's voice said, "Gordon? Come on in," which confirmed my deduction that she was in the staffroom already, don't you agree?

As no one immediately filled the chair vacated by Gordon, beside me, I was left to my own devices for a little while, and the sandwiches had revived me somewhat so I wasn't nearly so drowsy as I might have been and had some time to order my thoughts and try to decide who exactly might be the murderer in our midst.

I wasn't at all afraid, despite the knowledge that I was locked in a hair salon with a cold-blooded killer, because it seemed perfectly apparent that whilst everybody had a strong dislike for the poor deceased man, no one in the salon seemed to dislike anyone else present, at least as far as I could tell, and if we discount the general distaste some of us felt towards Dougal Rufus, that is, or the little spat between Flora and Alice which seemed to have been all but forgotten in the wake of the day's drama. Dennis did ask me about that afterwards, and wondered why I hadn't been most terribly scared, but it wasn't like that at all, and no one in the salon showed any notions of wanting to kill *me*, even without Amity there to protect me.

I let the chatter wash over me, keeping one ear cocked for any useful snippets or clues, but mostly I was content to let my mind drift. Often, one finds thoughts come along quite uninvited at times of relaxation, much as at the exact moment one tries to go to sleep, the brain decides to instigate a conversation about the early works of William Shakespeare or whether you have remembered to take some meat out of the freezer to defrost. It was the same in those quiet minutes in the salon, and I must say I reached some very interesting conclusions and by the time Alice handed me yet another cup of tea and sat beside me to drink her own, I was without doubt that I had narrowed the suspects to four.

Chapter Fourteen

Unfortunately, I was interrupted from expanding on such things as means and motives and narrowing the pool of suspects further by the unwelcome aroma of cigarettes and body odour. If this were not clue enough, the squeak of Dougal Finbury's shoes announced his unbidden arrival into my personal space.

He stopped inches from my chair, throwing me into darkness and causing a slight shiver to run through my body. The man really could benefit from some extra training in people skills. I would suggest it to that lovely D.S. Nasir at the first opportunity.

"Mrs Smith? They. Need. To. Talk. To. You. Come with me." He addressed me in the manner of one talking to a small child who had drawn on the living room walls in permanent marker pen, but I have never taken that kind of nonsense from anyone and as I swung my feet from the footrest, I may have accidentally jabbed him with my toe. It's terribly difficult to know exactly where someone's shin is, when you can't see, so accidents invariably happen.

Of course, if a person is standing close enough that one can feel their stagnant breath on your cheek, one can be reasonably certain one's foot would make contact *somewhere* about their person. The silly boy.

"Oof," he muttered, and stepped mercifully backwards, allowing the space around me to brighten by several literal shades and innumerable metaphorical shades.

I fumbled for my cane and got to my feet.

He grabbed my arm much as one might grab a cat that is about to relieve itself in one's flowerbed and I shook him off.

"I can manage perfectly well, thank you very much. Tell me where I am needed and I will make my way. If I need assistance, I shall ask Alice, who is quite adept at guiding the visually impaired without any of this heavy-handed manhandling."

With that, I followed him to the staffroom—a small room I hadn't entered before, but which, as I had already gathered, contained the kettle and tea-making facilities and smelled of coffee and hairspray.

"Ah, Mrs Smith," said the soft voice of D.S. Nasir. "Would you like me to guide you to a seat?" She has a lovely way about her. Proper manners, such as one should expect from an officer of the law.

I accepted her help graciously and she tucked my hand gently into her arm.

"Three large steps forward, and there is a comfortable chair to your right. There now." She guided my hand to touch the arm of the chair. It was velvet-soft and not at all sticky or roughened. A sure indication of a high-end staffroom. Claude is an employer who appreciates his staff. Or perhaps he is just finicky in his interior design tastes, but one can be both, I suppose. The coffee is the good kind of coffee, too. Not that instant-in-a-jar chicory full of unpleasant lumps where damp spoons have been inserted, that you find in so many school staffrooms.

I patted my way into what seemed to be one of those strangely-named tub chairs and settled myself against its cushioned back. D.S. Nasir was correct; the seat was indeed pleasingly comfortable, and offered good lumbar support to boot.

"Thank you, Constable Finbury." Her tone was dismissive and it was easy to infer her feelings towards the reprobate. The door closed with a sharp click as he left the room, as if he had pulled it with a little petulant force, and the invigorating aroma of Claude's high-quality coffee machine replaced the pungent whiff of Dougal Rufus.

"How can I help?" I said to my new friend.

Over the course of a cup of tea—in a perfectly acceptable mug, God bless the woman—and two Bourbon Cream biscuits, which were very welcome, I relayed how I had accidentally stumbled into the cleaning cupboard after mistaking it for the lavatory and discovered what I had presumed to be a heap of soiled laundry.

"Oh come now, Mrs Smith," D.S. Nasir chided me gently. Really, she would have made a most excellent teacher. "You and I both know it was no accident. Claude tells me you are more than capable of navigating the salon, and even had he not, I have seen for myself that you are not as doddery as you like to pretend when it suits you."

I rewarded her with a small chuckle. She is encouragingly observant.

"Talk me through what you noticed and why you felt it necessary to venture into the cupboard." The light shifted fractionally and I sensed her settle against the back of her chair. I wondered whether her seat matched my own, or whether Claude liked to mix it up.

"What colour are the chairs?" I asked D.S. Nasir, and to her credit, she was happy to indulge my curiosity, and I added mustard-yellow-with-cerise-cushions to my mental image of the room. Her seat, she informed me, was a bench-style sofa, rigid in looks, but supportive and comfortable. Three seats. Matching velvet upholstery. Dimpled with those little buttons. She is extremely good at details, and I told her so.

"I'm supposed to notice detail," she said. "It's my job."

I discerned a hint of pride in her voice, nevertheless.

Having established some level of rapport and mutual understanding, I had no qualms in sharing my observations.

In return, she shared some of her own.

Robert J. Robertson, I assured her, had not entered the salon during the time in which I had been present therein.

"Would it be possible that he came in while you visited the ladies' at any point? Or that you wouldn't have heard him enter if you had your earphones in? What were you listening to?"

I explained to the lovely detective that I had not visited the lavatory prior to the occasion on which I discovered the body, and also that I am perfectly capable of noticing more than one sound at a time. Even at such times during which I utilise my earphones, and might be thoroughly engrossed in a gripping story, I have, by necessity, become adept at simultaneously keeping my ears open to other events.

"My grandson," I informed her, "calls it my Spidey senses. Besides, even in the unlikely instance I had not heard anyone enter, I would have felt the air as the door opened. Especially on a day as cold as this." I relayed to the detective the comings and goings of the afternoon, and I think she was both convinced and impressed.

Phyllis and I had entered at the same time, at one o'clock precisely, which I could corroborate by the chime of the town clock as well as by Flora, who had greeted us with a perfunctory "Come in," after she unlocked the door to admit us onto the premises.

"Unlocked it?" D.S. Nasir's voice affected surprise, although she certainly would have been party to this information already.

"I am quite sure Claude or Alice or Bobby-Jo or Gordon or even Lily or Flora has informed you that between the hours of twelve and one, the salon closes for lunch. You are most definitely not surprised that someone had to unlock the door to allow the first of the afternoon's clients to enter."

"True," she conceded, "but indulge me. Please continue as if I have not yet interviewed anyone else at all."

"I see," I said. "You wish to find plot holes and loopholes and inconsistencies."

"Yes."

"Then I shall do my best to help you find some."

For the main part of my regaling the sequence of events, D.S. Nasir allowed me to speak without interruption. Now and then, she may interject a question, and at one point she refilled my cup and offered me another biscuit, which I graciously declined, although I am partial to a Bourbon Cream and we rarely have them at home, what with Dennis's cholesterol and my limitations.

Maud had been inside the salon already. As Claude had ushered me and Phyllis inside, and relieved us of our coats in a most chivalrous manner, Alice had called, "With you in a minute Mrs Smith! Just getting a cuppa for Gran," which was how I became aware of Maud's presence therein. I had, I explained to the Detective Sergeant, attempted to greet the woman at that time, but my words had gone unheard. Maud and I had, however, exchanged greetings a little while later, at such time as I first visited the ladies' room, as it turned out that she, too, had availed of a little comfort break. I hadn't stopped to chat, due to the pressing on my bladder and then, on my way back, I had quite forgotten about Maud, due to the smell in the cupboard. Maud wouldn't have noticed the smell. She has no need to rely on her sense of smell to tell her things, as her eyes still function perfectly well although I suspect she is a wearer of spectacles, these days.

"It's naughty of you have spent the afternoon pretending you need help to find your way to the toilets, Mrs Smith," said the D.S., and although she tried to sound stern, I caught the tiniest hint of laughter in her tone. "Given that you were managing to get there and back quite well without help when you discovered the body."

"I must admit, I wondered if anyone had noticed," I said, without apology. "It's been most terribly boring with nothing to do all afternoon and not even my audiobook to listen to with my device confiscated and whatnot. I'm sure you forgive a need for communication when I am unable to see what's been going on and that imbecilic Dougal Rufus prevented us from chattering in our seats."

"Quite," she said, and that was that, as she quickly returned to the more pressing matters in the retelling of the afternoon's events. "If a customer was already in the salon, why was the door still locked when you arrived?"

I said I had at first imagined that Maud had arrived a little early and due to her family connections, Alice had let her in, but Alice had later explained the reasons with more accuracy, and that Maud, after leaving the café in which they had enjoyed their lunch, had developed a pressing need to urinate and Alice had brought her to the salon a little earlier than either had expected. "I am quite certain both Maud and Alice have relayed this to you," I said to the Detective Sergeant.

"Indeed they have," she agreed, which was reassuring as my memory is not always what it used to be, and although I was certain of this information, it is always encouraging to have my recollections confirmed, especially by a proper detective.

"One might be forgiven for concluding that Maud's bladder has a lot to answer for," I said, "but as a woman of advancing years, I can sympathise completely."

"That would be a perfectly plausible reason, for sure," D.S. Nasir agreed, and I wondered if she might be sucking at the end of her pen although she seemed too well-presented to do anything so unhygienic as that.

"It would," I continued. "As you have clearly noticed, I have had a significant amount of time to chat with Alice during the afternoon, and I can tell you that Maud and Alice had lunch together before returning to the salon a little before one. Alice and Maud were together for the duration of the salon's lunch hour and I imagine that if you were to dispatch Dougal Finbury to the café, someone would be able to corroborate that information. As long as he asks nicely and doesn't get their back up before he starts."

D.S. Nasir gave a little sniff and I would bet my new hair colour that she was concealing a laugh.

"Which of the cafés?"

I was a bit stumped by that, as I couldn't be sure whether Alice had said, but as soon as I gave the matter some thought, I presumed she meant The Tea Cup, as Bread and Breakfast is really more of a coffee shop attached to the bakery, and is, as its name suggests, entirely better suited to breakfasts than to lunch and not at all the kind of place Maud would wish to partake of a nice lunch with her granddaughter in the week before Christmas. I said as much to the Detective Sergeant and she admitted that, yes, Alice and Maud had both said they had been in The Tea Cup, and enjoyed a lovely window seat overlooking the park, so she'd known the answer to her question all along, and once again I was reminded of the similarity between being a detective and being a teacher.

I said I couldn't imagine there had been much to look at in the park, as it was a cold, dull day in December, but that was hardly the point. "But, unfortunately," I added, "they must both still be considered amongst your prime suspects."

"Why do you say that?"

"I think it is safe to say, Detective Sergeant Nasir, that you are looking at a very short list of possible culprits. I am certain that the murderer can only be one of four, and of those, I would much prefer not to believe any of them are capable of such a thing." I took a fortifying swig of my tea while I gathered my wits. I very much did not want to believe in the evidence, but as is often the way of these occasions, had little choice but to speak out.

"Go on."

"I am terribly sorry to say so, but your culprit is most certainly Claude, Gord, Alice, or Maud." I sighed. "I dearly wish to be wrong on this occasion, but I believe I will be proved correct."

She must have shifted in her seat, because she rested a gentle hand on my knee as a waft of jasmine prickled my nose. "Talk me through it, Sally, as clearly and concisely as you are able."

Rather than finding her familiarity unwanted, her use of my first name was reassuring and comforting. Sana Nasir, my instincts assured me, was a police officer I could trust to listen carefully; consider my words, and act upon my observations. I took a deep breath to steady myself, and told her my theory.

Chapter Fifteen

"As Alice had not been quite ready for me," I told the D.S., "what with seeing to Maud's tea and whatnot, I spent a few moments chatting with Claude as he settled me into my seat. He confirmed the details of my appointment, of course, by asking about my hair."

In the manner of all good stylists, he'd stood behind me as we talked, lifting strands from my head and running my locks through his fingers. I recall from days gone by how a stylist might watch their client in the mirror, thus seeing their face as the client would see it herself, so I imagine Claude was doing just that.

"A little tint will certainly jazz you up for Christmas, Mrs S.," he'd said, and patted my scalp gently with his fingertips. "Not that you need any jazzing up. You're still quite the looker, Mrs S., I'll bet you and Phyllis turn all the heads when you're out on the town."

I expect I retorted with something along the lines of, "Oh don't be such a silly, Claude," but of course I was flattered all the same. It's his job, of course, to make his clients feel good about themselves, but he says it in such a thoroughly convincing manner.

I asked him had he had a good lunch, and he told me he was a little rushed as he was just tidying up some stray bottles before leaving when the telephone rang, and as everyone else had already dashed out to squeeze every second out of their lunch hour, he'd answered it.

"I should have let it go to voicemail, but I can never let a phone go unanswered," he'd said, with a trace of wry humour in his voice. "I'm too nosy for my own good, my mother always says, and honestly, Mrs S., I wished I hadn't because there's only so much a man needs to know about a child's gippy tummy and she could have just told the voicemail she couldn't come in for her hair tomorrow without all the gory details if I'd only left it to ring out." He wiggled his fingertips in my hair and I responded with a mock shudder and a little giggle.

"Ooh, you poor man, and just before your lunch, too."

He made the kind of snorting noise that sounds like one of those little pug dogs with the squashed-up faces, so I knew he was seeing the funny side of things as he regaled me with the story. He'd lost a good fifteen minutes of his lunch time, he said, because just as he thought he was about to finally get away and meet Gordon in the pub, Flora had come in, in quite a panic, looking for her bank card, and then he'd added that I was lucky he'd managed to return to the salon for one o'clock, after being so late getting away for his lunch, or we'd not have had time for that lovely little chat while I waited for Alice.

As soon as it became apparent it was a *body* that lay so odorously in the cleaning cupboard and not merely a pile of soiled towels or suchlike, I'd recalled not only that Claude had admitted to having been alone in the salon, but also that he had planted another useful clue into our conversation. He'd told me he was glad that the delivery they'd been waiting for hadn't decided to arrive during that time, even though he wished it would hurry up, otherwise he'd never have got away, and we'd have all been party to the rumblings of his stomach throughout the rest of the afternoon.

"As it was," he'd grumbled, "I only had time to gobble down my BLT with a glass of lemonade, and if Gord hadn't ordered it for me, I'd have had no lunch at all!" He'd added a little harumphing sound at that, and his fingers had stilled in my hair as he'd imagined the horrors of a lunch hour without lunch. "I almost didn't mind that Gordy had eaten half of it by the time I got to him, but that's between you and me, Mrs S., and don't you dare tell him. I'm not going to lie to you, Mrs S.; I was gagging for a glass of wine by then. Gagging, I tell you. It's been busy all morning and it's close enough to Christmas to drink at lunchtime, right?"

I'd chuckled along with him, not faulting his logic. I don't mind a lunchtime tipple myself and I had very much been looking forward to a leisurely afternoon tea with Phyllis after we left the salon, during which we would almost certainly have indulged in a little glass of something ourselves, to celebrate. I relayed all this to the delightful Detective Sergeant, and she laughed sympathetically and said she was sorry our afternoon treat had been ruined.

"Counting the hours until closing time, he was," I told D.S. Nasir, returning to the subject of Claude. "Can't say I blame him, but maybe it was a premonition." I paused for a moment to allow my next words their full impact. "Or perhaps he was, in his own words, *gagging* for a stiff drink because while the salon was empty of staff and clients, the delivery did in fact arrive, and by the time Claude joined Gordon in the pub, he had just clonked a man over the head and left him breathing his last in the broom cupboard."

D.S. Nasir did interrupt me then, to point out that being alone for fifteen minutes might put Claude in a compromising position but was not reason enough to deduce that he had actually killed a man, especially one who, according to Claude, was not even there.

I waved my hand in a vague dismissive gesture. "That is quite true," I agreed, "but until you are quite certain as to the time the unfortunate man did arrive, you cannot be sure whom amongst your suspects is telling the truth and who is not."

During the hours in which I had been largely confined to my faux-leather salon chair, I had gleaned many snippets of information, one of which was to ascertain that Robert J. Robertson had most definitely not arrived with his delivery during the morning's opening hours. Each member of staff had corroborated this fact in the chaotic and panic-laden interim between Alice's discovery of the body and the arrival of the incompetent Doofus Finbury, and it had been affirmed many times throughout the ensuing chatter of the afternoon. I can be quite certain of this, as in those moments of fluster and confusion immediately after the body was discovered, several people shared a common refrain: "When did he come in? I didn't even know he'd arrived."

Bobby-Jo had been particularly annoyed, as she'd been waiting for a certain brand of conditioning oil and had to explain to her client that it hadn't yet arrived. "And you're telling me it's been there in the cupboard all afternoon," she'd said in a most disgruntled tone that carried across the salon during one lull in the buzz of other conversations.

"Yes, along with a dead body, which seems a little more important, don't you think?" Gordon had retorted quite sharply, but it was a valid observation, and I didn't hear Bobby-Jo complain about the conditioning oil again after that.

"Well," she'd said huffily, "it wasn't there at quarter to eleven, because I had a few minutes spare after finishing my nine o'clock before heading out to the nativity so I went to get it ready for Tilly's appointment and it wasn't there and I do think I would have noticed if I had stepped over a dead delivery man to look, don't you?" Tilly, who is a sweet young thing who works in the Spar, was one of the clients who had come in and out between my arrival and the discovery of the body, and I haven't mentioned her before as she is entirely unimportant to the matter in hand.

Gordon had gone a bit quiet at that and moved out of my earshot, but Lily had piped up in agreement, saying she'd emptied a pan-load of sweepings into the big bin in there just before leaving for lunch, and if he'd been there then, they'd have had two dead bodies to worry about because she knew, just knew, she'd have died of the shock of it all and she'd never seen a dead body before and wasn't it just so awful and then she'd burst into noisy, snivelling tears and for the next few minutes the only sound in the whole place were her sobs and the others trying to calm her down. They'd managed, in the end, but Lily's only a young thing, and I don't think she'd be able to fake that level of hysteria.

Once Lily had calmed down, there was a bit of discussion about who had last been into the cupboard, aside from me, that is, or Alice, when she went it to find out about the smell. You might think that would mean Alice was off the hook, and I did wish I could have believed that was true, but unfortunately, she couldn't be, because she and Maud had been alone in the salon for several minutes during the pertinent window of time, and if you remember, Alice had claimed to be making her grandmother a cup of tea when Phyllis and I showed up for our appointments and Flora let us in, and as Claude and Gordon and Flora all claimed to have only just returned to the salon themselves, a minute or so before Phyllis and I arrived, it seems that Alice was alone in the staffroom and Maud was alone in the main part of the salon for at least a few minutes during the lunch period, and no one can be entirely confident that it was not during those few minutes that the delivery arrived, although I cannot imagine Maud would have been the one to unlock the door and admit him into the salon.

"One must also," I said, "not underestimate the loyalty a grandmother might feel towards her granddaughter, or vice versa. They may be corroborating the same story but that does not mean both or either are telling the *truth*."

Thus at the time at which Phyl and I were admitted into the salon, Claude, Gord, Alice and Maud were present within. And Flora, who'd admitted us into the salon, as I have said. She did not help me navigate the entryway, but retreated immediately behind the counter as the telephone rang. Nonetheless, Phyllis guided me across the threshold, and she is so much more used to assisting me than Flora, so it worked out perfectly well and I did not collide with the doorframe or indeed the potted plant, although I believe

Claude may have relocated the plant after the unfortunate incident in June.

I shuddered a little as I remembered about that, and D.S. Nasir clucked sympathetically and asked if I'd been hurt, and I said not very much and I'd got over it well enough and then I said I'd better continue with telling her the events of the afternoon in question so as not to get distracted.

"Yes, do go on, you're doing very well," she said, so I did.

By the time Claude helped me out of my overcoat, Flora was already speaking on the telephone. I'm entirely certain she had the contraption tucked between her ear and her shoulder, so she could file her nails or skim through the appointment book, or tap away at her keypad to enter details on the computer, although the noise of her speaking, and Claude speaking, and Phyllis and me speaking, and Alice calling out about the tea, all overwhelmed my hearing somewhat and would have drowned out any little background sounds like keyboard-tapping or the like.

A little while later, while Claude and I were chatting, she did call out something to Claude about having ordered the frangipani, so perhaps it had been the florist on the telephone. I do have excellent hearing, but eavesdropping on a salon receptionist's telephone habits had not been my priority. I may need to utilise the full extent of my hearing to find my bearings and get around, but I'm not a *nosy* woman.

"The point of this observation," I assured the D.S., "is merely to ascertain that Flora, like Claude, Gordon, Alice, and Maud, was there."

"Yes," she said, in her calm, even voice, so she seemed appreciative of my attention to detail.

Flora, however, seemed to have enough of an alibi regardless of to whom she spoke on the telephone, as everyone was in agreement that Claude had been with her while she rummaged for her bank card, and Gordon has seen her enter and leave within five minutes or so, from his vantage point in the window table in the pub.

I had no reason not to believe Claude when he said he was alone in the salon between approximately twelve-noon and twelve-fifteen, but even if this were not the case, and he was lying, there would remain the question of why he would lie about being there if he had not. It would be perfectly understandable if he were to say he had *not* been alone in the salon at that time, in order to put himself in the clear, as it were, but to lie about being there if he was not, is certainly not to anyone's advantage. Except the killer's, of course. Nonetheless, the times he gave were supported by Gordon and Flora, which certainly added weight to Claude's side of the story. However, this honesty cannot let him slide from the hook, as the fact remains that he was in the right place at the right time however one looks at it.

"Unless I am very much mistaken," I said in the general direction of D.S. Nasir, who had not spoken for a while but had also not moved from her seat, "we have a very finite window of opportunity, during which time not only did the poor man arrive with his delivery but during which time someone also murdered him."

"Yes," she said, which I took as affirmation that the timing of the crime was indeed confined to that of the salon's lunchtime closing hour.

"And, if I am correct in my suspicions, no one has, thus far, confessed to knowing he had arrived, or to meeting him, or to bashing him on the head."

"Yes," she said. "No. No one admits to having seen him."

"But," I went on, "it also seems apparent that he may not, in fact, have been *bashed*."

I imagine she raised her eyebrows and turned upon me with a questioning gaze, but of course I cannot know this for sure.

I regaled to Detective Sergeant Nasir the incongruities of Alice's description of the body, even allowing for the girl's obvious distress. "How," I asked, "could Alice have recognised the man with such certainty, given that she also said his head had been bashed in? Had he been lying face up, you may find this plausible, but not for very long."

"Go on," the D.S. said.

"Well," I said, "one would imagine that in order to successfully kill a man by bashing him on the head, you would need some element of surprise or superior strength. With the possible exception of Gordon, who is a tall man with a muscular physique, I find it hard to imagine any of your other suspects capable of strength enough to kill a man with a single blow to his face, or even to knock him out. Then we must also consider that there was sufficient blood to cause a rather pongy smell, implying significant bleeding. Were the bleeding to the front of his head, and his head as 'bashed in' as Alice led me to think, his face would be difficult to recognise with such certainty as Alice provided."

"Mmhm," D.S. Nasir said, but as she said no more than that, I took this as indication to continue.

"It is, I should think, more likely that in order for any of our suspects to successfully bash in a man's head, they would have come up behind him and taken him by surprise. If this were the case, he would likely also fall forward, onto his face, thus obscuring his most recognisable features. Alice may, of course, have registered some familiar clothing or shoes, given her past relationship with the man, but that in itself would not be as conclusive as her manner suggested. There were only seconds between her going to investigate the smell and her scream, and her scream brought her colleagues to the scene within an equally small number of seconds. She told me Claude pushed her aside from the doorway in order to see what she was screaming about, so it is reasonable to deduce that she had less than sixty seconds to take in the situation and accurately identify the man."

I paused for a moment to take a little sip of my tea and organise my thoughts before continuing with my deductions.

"Are you all right, Mrs Smith? Still have plenty of tea? Would you like a glass of water."

I agreed that as I had a lot more to say on the matter, some water would be most welcome, so we had a little interlude whilst the detective got to her feet, found a glass, and turned on the tap. She allowed it to run into the sink for a moment before filling the glass. I do prefer to allow the tap to run fully cold to ensure the water is palatable, and that she thought to do so without my asking, once again proved to me just how thorough and competent Detective Sergeant Sana Nasir is.

"Here you are." She put the water into my hand, then guided my hand to the low table beside the chair in which I sat, and helped me to set the glass just so, so I would know exactly where to place my hand in order to retrieve the glass at such time as I may need to take a sip. She really is terribly thoughtful and I meant to ask her if she has experience with the visually impaired, but I didn't want to get sidetracked from the matter in hand so filed away that question for later. She returned to the mustard-yellow sofa with the cerise cushions, and settled into her seat with a soft squooshing sound, then instructed me to continue if I were ready to do so, which of course I was, but I appreciated the little interlude, nonetheless.

"Well, then," I said, gathering my thoughts and regaining my place in the story. "We also have the problem that there was little within the cupboard of suitable weight and size for killing a man by hitting him on the head, and even were there an object suited to the purpose, the killer, unless already in the cupboard ahead of Mr Robertson, would have needed to manoeuvre around him in order to select the weapon, turn around in the confined space, and kill him. I also believe, from Alice's description of the situation, that his legs were nearer the door and his head furthest into the cupboard. The killer, if he were bashed about the head, was behind him, in the doorway, and not in the cupboard beyond the body, or he would, I believe, have toppled in the other direction. One tends to topple *away*, not *towards*, don't you agree?"

"I do," she said. "It is remarkably difficult to have a victim topple towards you, especially without them falling into you and covering you in blood, in my experience." She laughed, and I laughed too, because although we were talking of a very serious matter, she said this in such a tone that was quite amusing to us both, especially as I also imagined the entire scenario as a short cine-film spooling in my mind and it really was quite comical.

"So," she said, "I do tend to agree with you that the deceased would have most likely fallen away from the perpetrator. Go on, if you don't mind."

"I am therefore supposing two things, of which one or both must be true. The first of these is that Robert J. Robertson was not bashed on the head but killed in some other way. The second is that Alice knew who the dead man was without needing to identify him."

I recalled that Alice had said there was a remarkable amount of blood on the front of the man's clothing, and paused again for a moment to consider my next words before giving them voice. "Given the amount of blood and the contents of not only the cupboard but the main salon and potentially every stylist's pockets, I would speculate the murder weapon could, quite conceivably, have been a sharp pair of hairdressing scissors. A sharp jab to the neck would produce death with far less physical strength than a blow to the head, and result in a far larger flow of blood around the body, too, producing that metallic smell that stopped me in my tracks on my way to the ladies' at two-thirty-six this afternoon. Even a short person can manage a sharp upward thrust into a person's neck, might one assume?"

"Mmhm," the D.S. said, in a tone that I interpreted as agreement.

"But," I said, "there was no sign of a struggle, otherwise items would have fallen from the shelves. The room, if I may generously call it that, is small. As I tapped my cane about the floor, it made contact with the wall on either side, or possibly a run of cupboards such as one would find in a domestic kitchen, without moving from my position just inside the door. As the cupboard is situated alongside the lavatories, I would hazard a guess it is of equal depth to its neighbouring space—the depth of a small lobby containing a washbasin and hand dryer, with a small but adequate toilet cubicle beyond. I would be unsurprised to hear that the two spaces—the cupboard and the lavatory including the hand-wash area—are the same size in footprint. Quite enough room for a man's body to fall and for someone to shut the door behind him."

"Yes," the Detective Sergeant confirmed. "It is about the same size as the ladies' lavatory. You are indeed as astute as I suspected, Sally Smith."

"*Was* he stabbed?"

She was silent for a long moment, in which I took up the glass of water and had a drink. My mouth was getting quite dry by that time. I am unaccustomed, these days, to talking at such length, although in my teaching days I would often talk for a good forty minutes or so, especially in History classes, which tends to be a subject in which many secondary school pupils are prone to drifting off; wasting the lessons in gazing out of the windows and yawning, and executing a distinct lack of participation. I must confess I found English Literature classes altogether more rewarding, throughout my time at St Cuthbert's. I have quite the affinity with literature, but a chronic dislike of mathematics which just goes to show one doesn't need to be good at everything to have a successful teaching career.

"Are you proficient in mathematics?" I asked the detective, in order to fill the silence, although I supposed she must be, having confirmed the size of the cupboard so rapidly.

She gave a little chuckle. "A-level maths, physics, and biology."

"I thought as much. You are a credit to your teachers."

"Thank you," she said, and then after another brief pause, she added, "Yes. He was stabbed. In the neck. Exactly as you suggested. Are you quite sure it is not you we should be arresting, Mrs Smith?"

Chapter Sixteen

I was quick to reassure the Detective Sergeant that she was correct in her deduction, and I was most certainly not her perpetrator, and in return, she was quick to reassure me that she had no doubt in her mind pertaining to my innocence in the matter.

At this, I ventured to ask her for clarification of the reasons for continuing to detain us all, especially those of us who were irrefutably without guilt or opportunity such as Phyllis and Bobby-Jo, for starters.

Her explanation was much as I had already suspected: they wished to contain the spread of gossip and conjecture, whilst ensuring the real culprit not be inadvertently permitted to slip through their fingers and get away, which sounded terribly dramatic and exciting but I also took to mean I *was*, in fact, still a suspect, albeit by virtue only of my presence in the salon that afternoon rather than through any logical deductions or suspicions.

I didn't correct the Detective Sergeant in this contradiction of her reassurance with the facts of the matter, as by then, I was quite enjoying the sleuthing with which I had begun to occupy my mind, and I was determined to solve the puzzle and aid the inquiries, as they say in the movies. (Phyllis did tell me afterwards that when one is aiding with inquiries, one is usually far more of a likely suspect than I was, and it is not entirely uncommon for those aiding with inquiries to become detained and request the presence of a solicitor before imparting any further information, so I suppose she was right about that, but I did like the sound of aiding the police, nevertheless, and that, in my opinion is what I did. I don't imagine my solicitor would be experienced in such matters as murder, now I think about it, as he usually deals with wills and legacies and transfers of property and divorces. He has a tiny office beneath Claude's apartment, as I think I may have mentioned.)

After the Detective Sergeant assured me she harboured no suspicions as to my involvement in the matter, she asked me to continue to recount my observations.

Bobby-Jo, I reminded her, had been at her son's nativity play, which I presumed had taken place in the school hall, just as it had for as long as I can remember.

"She has photographs on her telephone," I said, "and I imagine the device will tell you with a good deal of accuracy exactly what time the photographs were taken, so I imagine you have confirmed that with her by now and you are confident her alibi is solid, especially when you consider how long it would take her to get there and back." Little Wittering Primary School is a good fifteen minutes from Claude's Curls. One might expect it to be quicker in a car, but one must take into account the walk to the car park; the one-way system, and the roadworks by the Co-op.

"Did you happen to notice which of the Three Kings her son portrayed, and the gift he carried? I was being subjected to the hair-dryer and missed the conclusion of that enquiry."

D.S. Nasir chuckled at that and said he'd looked very cute with his gap-toothed grin and a gold-wrapped something-or-other, which was a roundabout way of letting me know she'd checked the photographs and confirmed the alibi.

As she seemed willing to indulge my curiosity in return for my observations on the afternoon's events, I asked her whether Gordon had, in fact, visited the photographer as he had claimed, or if he had nipped back into the salon, admitted Robert J. Robertson, and stabbed him in the neck with a lethal weapon. I also asked her if it had been concluded whether the van Claude had seen parked outside the Bread and Breakfast was, indeed, Robertson's delivery van, and at what time it had been parked there.

Detective Sergeant Nasir agreed that the van spotted outside the bakery *was* that belonging to the newly-deceased Robertson, and it had now been towed away, which I knew already from Finbury's comments, but not that it had been the same van as that spotted by Claude from the pub window.

"I presume," I said, "that Claude and Gordon took their lunch in the Grape and Hop and not The Leaky Tap?"

"Go on," D.S. Nasir said. "Tell me why you presume that."

"Gordon said he saw Flora go back for her bank card. One simply can't see the salon from The Leaky Tap, however good one's eyesight might be. The Grape is almost opposite, and offers a direct line of sight, for those with such blessings intact." Besides, I thought but did not say aloud, the Grape is an altogether classier place, as pretentious and clean as its name might suggest, and perfectly suited to such an elegant couple as Claude and Gordon. The Leaky Tap smells predominantly of beer and sweat and tends to have a terribly sticky floor, although I rarely go in, nowadays, so perhaps it has changed.

"You're right, of course," she said, with a little smile in her voice.

"It is imperative to discover which of Little Wittering's many photographers Gordon claims to have visited, and to confirm that he arrived at such photographic studios at around about the time he claims."

"Just a moment; yes," she said, and I thought she must be looking at her notes or her telephone screen. "P.C. Finbury is on it," she added without much of a pause so she must have had the information at her fingertips, although she didn't share it with me.

"Dear Claude is most concerned," I said. "Gordon did not do as Claude had expected, which has allowed a niggle of uncertainty to ease its way into Claude's mind. I do hope someone has managed to attend to Pumpkin, poor little poppet. Gordon, too, is shouldering the weight of doubt, as he is concerned that *Claude* had opportunity and motive, given his presence in the salon for approximately fifteen minutes after everyone else had left and before Flora returned to collect her bank card. Of course, if one of them did kill the unfortunate man, he will know the other did not, but there is no accounting for protecting one's loved ones in times of crisis, and it may take significant probing to persuade either man to formally accuse the other with any degree of conviction."

I felt about beside me for the water glass, and took a sip.

"Mmhm," the detective said, as if she were both agreeing and thinking. "So what about Flora, then?"

"Indeed. Flora initially fell under suspicion, of course, and she has not disputed her presence on the premises during the time in question."

"But you don't believe she's a suspect?"

I replaced my glass on the little table beside the chair. "I think it improbable, despite her obvious dislike of Robertson. Gordon saw her enter, and he also saw her leave a few minutes later, with Claude, and he watched Claude lock the door behind them and approach the pub. Flora, according to Gordon, went off at a great pace away from the salon, and although she may have ducked around a bit and then returned, it seems unlikely, don't you think? Why would she? She had found her bank card. Claude verifies both its loss and recovery, so that is without dispute. Claude and she both assure us Robertson did not arrive during the few minutes they were together in the salon. Even if she had gone back to confront the man, if he wasn't there, she would have had to wait, which may have been conspicuous, especially when one considers Claude had blown her excuse to return. All things considered, I can't imagine she would try again immediately, can you?"

The D.S. gave a little murmur of agreement and shifted in her seat. I imagined her leaning forward with her hands on her knees; a look of intense focus on an attractive but serious face, although she could just as easily have been gazing at her fingernails or playing a game on her telephone or any amount of minor, undecipherable activity, but I have the impression she is not like that at all so I had little doubt I held her full attention, and continued in my recollections.

"I suspect the Bread and Breakfast will be able to confirm her presence, either by recollection, or with more accuracy, via her payment transaction. It is indeed a blessing that she did retrieve her bank card, or Claude would have lent her the cash and there would be none of those funny electronic fingerprints one gets nowadays." My son is one of those people who understands computers and usually when he pops around to see us, Dennis collars him to assist with some newfangled installation on his personal computer, but I can't quite understand them myself although I must concede that they are terribly useful contraptions, don't you agree? "I trust your people have got onto that, also?" I said to D.S. Nasir.

"Did she tell you she was in the Bread and Breakfast?"

"She did not, but I am quite certain she was in that particular establishment, Detective Sergeant Nasir, on several counts." I raised my index finger, as if testing for the direction of the wind. "One, given her hostilities with Alice, it is unlikely she chose to take her lunch hour in the same café as Alice and Maud, who have separately informed me of their view over the park on this rather dull day, which locates them in The Tea Cup, as that is the only eatery with a view over the park in December." There is a little café inside the park, beside the lake, but it is seasonal and won't be open again until March or April, I shouldn't think.

I held up a second finger, keeping track for myself as much as for the police officer. "Two, she mentioned to Claude that she had ordered in frangipani, as per his request, and I couldn't imagine why he needed more flowers given there is already a plethora of Christmas decorations around the salon, including a potted Christmas tree taking up what Annabel described as 'half the counter', but now I've had time to think about it, I imagine she meant frangipane, and I think you'll find the bakery produces the most exquisite frangipane. The Tea Cup is more inclined to cupcakes and Victoria sponge and tends not to dabble in pastries. Or takeaway items."

I took another sip of water and cast my unseeing eyes in the direction of the Detective Sergeant. Once I had set down the glass, I raised a third finger. "The bakery also has a far more selective array of coffees than does The Tea Cup, as one might expect, and Flora had the faintest whiff of stale coffee breath when she came to sit beside me." I broke off as I sensed the detective lean forward on Claude's mustard-coloured sofa, but I held up my hand to placate her, raising my remaining fingers into a gesture of 'wait'. "Which in itself is inconclusive, of course, and one may get coffee elsewhere, but I don't believe Flora made herself coffee in the staffroom in the salon during the hour or so before the incident, as after admitting Phyllis and me, she remained at the desk attending to telephone calls, breaking from that only to greet clients as they arrived; chat to that young lad from Luigi's who popped in with a flyer, according to Phyllis, and to file her nails. She did not leave her position until the body was discovered, unless she slipped into the staffroom in the few minutes in which I visited the lavatory, but Phyllis didn't say so and Phyllis is quite reliable in such matters. Aside from all that, one may also conclude that The Tea Cup is really too far for Flora to have got there and back in the time span, given that Gordon and Claude have both agreed she was back in the salon at approximately ten past twelve. To have had time to get to The Tea Cup, place her order, realise her card was missing, and return to search for it, all within ten minutes, would be pushing it, as I believe they say nowadays. I doubt she would have bothered, to be perfectly frank."

"You are correct, of course. And the bakery have confirmed it exactly as you say."

There was a brief lull in our conversation while the D.S. tapped at her screen with the pads of her fingers. She really is a most practical kind of woman, as there was none of that ridiculous clickety noise one gets if one has those modern kinds of fingernails, such as Flora seems to have. When Flora taps at a screen, the clicking is quite incessant and I can only wonder how she manages to get anything done. Perhaps that is why she didn't become a hair stylist, now I think about it.

"Eleven-pounds-seventy-eight. Ham and cheese croissant and two espressos," said the D.S, which stopped me thinking about Flora's nails and brought me back quite sharply to the matter in hand. "And she placed an order for a frangipane tart, divided into eight equal slices, for Claude to collect in the morning. Hmm. I am impressed, Sally. Most impressed. I am also inclined to agree with you. Flora is not our priority."

Chapter Seventeen

I was as reluctant to give voice to the possibility that Alice or Maud were likely suspects as I had been to consider Claude or Gordon, but the evidence indicated that one of the four must be so. I sighed quite heavily, before continuing, worried that once I emitted the words, they would be irretrievable.

D.S. Nasir leaned towards me and rested her hand gently on my forearm for a second. "Go on," she said, in a voice as soft and kind as that luxurious triple-ply velvet toilet tissue Claude gets in for his clientele. Dennis and I usually stick to the two-ply; three-ply seems terribly extravagant and a little pretentious to boot, don't you find?

"You must understand," I said, pushing away my incongruous thoughts of lavatory paper, "that I do not wish *any* of these people to be a murderer, and it is with great regret that I have reached my conclusions."

"I know," she said, patting my arm and withdrawing her hand. "I know. It is an unfortunate part of my job to realise that often, the most ordinary and likeable people sometimes commit the most terrible crimes."

"I suppose anyone can have a lapse of judgement. Act irrationally in a moment of provocation."

"Yes. You'd be surprised," she said, but her tone had a weary edge that suggested she was no longer surprised by anything at all.

"I suppose there is very little you haven't seen, in your position?" I hope I matched the sympathetic kindness she has demonstrated, and for a moment, I felt most terribly sorry for her.

"How about you tell me your thoughts, Sally, and then I can decide whether they are worth acting upon? It is always useful to have a second opinion, if only to clarify my own observations."

I whole-heartedly agreed with that sentiment, and it was the encouragement I needed to continue with my damning suspicions of at least one of the four most likely suspects.

"Alice and Maud appear to have the largest window of opportunity," I said, with a sigh. "There are, as I see it, several possibilities. Either Alice or Maud could have admitted the man to the salon and stabbed him as he delivered the goods to the cupboard, or one could have admitted him and the other stabbed him, or they could have tackled the man together. I don't think Maud would have admitted him to the salon, as she wouldn't have had a key—" As I voiced this to the detective, a new thought struck me, and I was surprised I hadn't considered it before. "—unless Alice had left the door unlocked, of course, and he strolled in without need of admission."

"Go on."

"She said she locked it, but one *would* say that, wouldn't one?"

"Yes," D.S. Nasir agreed, "I suppose she would."

"Phyllis said something I had not thought much of, until I had time to process my thoughts while everyone was busy with the sandwiches. She said that Maud's dress was a little damp, and she presumed she might have slopped her tea or some such misdemeanour. When we first arrived, that is. I didn't ask Phyllis to tell me *where* the dress was wet, as it hardly seemed important, but I do wonder now whether Maud may have washed blood from her clothing and not managed to dry it completely?" I paused and shook my head as if to clear the very idea from my mind. "I find it quite improbable that Maud would admit the man to the salon, accompany him to the cupboard, and brutally stab him, don't you? Even if one is to overlook Maud's advancing years and that she is a grandmother, it necessitates too many unlikely coincidences and factors, don't you think?"

"I do," D.S. Nasir agreed.

"And lacks any clarity of *motive*."

"Indeed."

"Unless ..." My little grey cells had, by then, had plenty of time to whirr and clunk, and the idea that was forming was one that necessitated not one of the four, but two of the four to have worked together to commit the dastardly deed. If Claude was covering for Gordon, or Gordon for Claude, the same logic might be applied to Maud and Alice, and while I had voiced this suggestion loosely, I had not yet put into words the scenario that spooled in my mind.

"Unless?"

"Unless Alice let him in, or he entered of his own accord, and then something happened—we know from Flora and Annabel and Alice that he was the kind of man who ...

encroached on a girls' personal space, so is it possible that he found Alice alone in the salon and ... attacked her?"

"He thought she was alone, you mean?"

"Yes. He wouldn't have expected Maud to be present, nor any of the other staff, during the lunch hour. Perhaps he was surprised to find anyone there to receive the delivery, but took advantage of his good fortune to try to win Alice back into his favour ... or, had she refused his advances, turned forceful." Even as I gave voice to the idea, I couldn't quite determine how this scenario could have played out. "But then, one would think, Alice would have said *something* to someone, wouldn't one? If he forced himself upon her and she acted to defend herself? Quite heroically, one could even venture, wouldn't you agree?"

"Hmm." D.S. Nasir must have got to her feet as I sensed the air move and the light dimmed just a fraction, then brightened again, dimmed and brightened, dimmed and brightened.

"Are you *pacing*, Detective?" I asked her, and she chuckled lightly and said, yes, she was.

"So, from what you say, we are looking at either Claude or Gordon, or Claude *and* Gordon, or Alice or Maud, or Alice *and* Maud as the only possible suspects?"

"I simply can't conceive of any other possibilities given the circumstances and the evidence," I said. "Can you?"

At that moment, somebody rapped on the door and, not waiting for permission to enter, Finbury barged into the room in his usual whiff of pomposity and Marlboros, and addressed the D.S. without invitation. You can tell a lot about a person by the way in which he enters a room, and I knew immediately it was Finbury by the rush of air created by the movement; the crashing of the door against the wall; the rapid footfall of the entrant, and the heavy breathing. A rhinoceros calf driving a bulldozer could have entered the room with more grace than Dougal Rufus.

I have also, since becoming visually-inconvenienced, noticed that there are certain types of people in the world who make the ludicrous presumption that one who is visually impaired is also either deaf or stupid or both, and Dougal Rufus Finbury is one such person, although one would think even an incompetent such as he should know better than to speak so freely about a murder investigation in the presence of a witness.

Nonetheless, he continued as if I were merely another armchair in the room, and announced with some grandiosity that Jill at Studio 8 in the Market Yard had confirmed Gordon had strolled into her photography studios at approximately twelve-forty-five, and she had told him she was terribly sorry but his frame had not yet arrived.

"The delivery, she said—" Finbury's words were loaded with so much self-importance I was sure his chest must be puffed out like a peacock in the throes of its mating ritual. "—had not yet arrived, although the delivery driver had phoned just before twelve to say he was on his way." Finbury coughed in fake modesty, as if he were awaiting applause.

I almost chuckled aloud as I envisaged him as one of those cartoon policemen from a Beano comic, perhaps hitching up his trousers, and I longed to turn conspiratorially to the Detective Sergeant and ask whether Doofus Finbury was wearing red braces and a large gold badge on his lapel saying

Sheriff but I did not wish to draw attention to my presence in case it brought Finbury to his senses and shut him up.

He did not shut up.

"Gordon then made two more telephone calls to Jill—"

Was he flicking through one of those little notebooks with spiral binding, and squinting at his badly-scrawled notes? His hand-writing had always left a lot to be desired and I must admit I couldn't believe for a moment it had improved, even with the benefit of Police Training College. Nevertheless, in the image formed in my mind, he studied his little notebook, and gave a little bob of his knees as he confirmed the time of the two telephone calls.

"He was in the shop for about five minutes, she thinks," Finbury blustered on. "She said they chatted for a minute or two before he left."

I had a childish urge to ask him whether it was five minutes or a minute or two, because what kind of a policeman contradicts the details of his report so carelessly in the space of a single sentence, but I held my tongue and the Detective Sergeant thanked him and he left the room.

The D.S. apologised for the interruption as the door emitted a gentle thud and closed behind the blundering constable.

I brushed away the apology, reminding her that I had once been Dougal Finbury's high school teacher and the only surprise to me was not his ineptitude in the job or his lack of social skills, but that he had managed to complete Police Training College in the first place. She didn't respond to that, which was further proof that she, in sharp contrast to her inferior colleague, is thoroughly professional.

Market Yard is home to a lovely little array of local craftspeople and artisans so I was pleased to hear that Gordon had supported one of them, however unsuccessful it had turned out to be. Jill is married to a terribly nice man named Jack, which has become quite the little joke around the townspeople, but as she will tell you, hadn't been quite enough to stop her marrying him.

"Market Yard," I said, "must be a good five-minute-walk, even for someone as energetic as Gordon." It would probably take me longer than that, even with Amity to guide me, so Finbury's information corroborated Gordon's story perfectly well, if you allowed him five minutes to walk in each direction. Even if he spent only a single minute chatting to the photographer, the dubious accuracy of Finbury's time-keeping seemed somewhat irrelevant. I simply couldn't imagine how even someone as tall and fit as Gordon could manage to lure a man inside the salon, entrap him in a cupboard, and kill him in less than three minutes, especially once one factors in that Gordon would have needed to also vacate the salon after the killing, in order to approach the front door from the High Street, and all without being seen by Alice or Maud who were in the salon at the time in question, or by Flora or Claude, who had arrived at the salon a little before one o'clock and would therefore have intercepted him on the doorstep.

"Yes," the Detective Sergeant agreed, and I suspected she was nodding slowly and thoughtfully as she, too, did the maths.

"Not Gordon," I said, as the D.S. sat down on the yellow sofa once more, marked by a little hissing squish as the cushions received her weight.

"I think," I said, "it would be interesting to hear a little more about why Alice looked as if she had been crying, don't you? And what exactly Maud had spilled on her shirt. And what Claude had been doing in the ten minutes during which he was alone in the salon before Flora came in for her bank card."

She didn't answer as such but muttered something about, "Telephone log ... telephone log ... ah yes ..." and although it seemed as though she was talking to herself, I gathered immediately that she was referring to the telephone call Claude claimed had detained him in the salon at approximately one o'clock that lunchtime and I was quite reassured to deduce she hadn't had any need to telephone the client who'd cancelled with her child's upset tummy and been spared from that rigmarole, at least.

"The nice thing," she said in her normal voice, "about modern technology, is that we no longer have to wait so long for phone records. You may not be aware, Sally, but the salon uses a mobile phone for its calls, and therefore, we can simply scroll through the call logs and find out exactly what calls were made or received at what time."

"I can never quite decide whether I approve of these new-fangled clever phones," I said. "It is true that they allow me so much more freedom, with all their confounding technological applications and whatnot, but I must confess I don't entirely approve of the need for a person to be *available* at every minute of the day." I tried to stifle a little huff of disapproval although I'm afraid I wasn't entirely successful in that, and D.S. Nasir gave a tiny chuckle of acknowledgement so perhaps she felt the same. "But I do concede that this modern advancement must be terribly convenient for you. I presume you are telling me in a roundabout way that you have been able to confirm or deny Claude's telephone conversation, although I don't suppose for a moment you will either confirm or deny any such thing to me!"

We had another little laugh and she was saved from answering by another knocking on the door—a sharp, purposeful knock this time; *rap-rap.* as if the perpetrator had something specific and important to impart and would brook no nonsense. Not Finbury, I'd have wagered my pension on that.

"Come in," the Detective Sergeant called and for the second time in a few minutes, the staffroom door was opened and not closed. I had the feeling that the new arrival was loitering on the threshold, neither entering nor retreating.

"May I have a word?" The voice was polite and deep and steady. Detective Inspector Nelson.

The D.S. got to her feet again with a creak of her knees that caused me to wonder if she might be a little older than I had imagined. "Excuse me, Mrs Smith," she said. "I'll just step outside for a moment to speak with D.I. Nelson. Will you be all right waiting there?"

She is most terribly attentive and I was pleased that she is the kind of person who tells me what I can't see for myself, as while I had recognised his voice, she wasn't to know that by any certain means. I assured her I would enjoy a moment of serenity alone in this comfortable room, and that she should take all the time she needed to get to the bottom of this unfortunate affair, and she left the room with the Inspector and the door was pulled shut behind them. However, the privacy was futile as they stood just beyond that closed door and had quite under-estimated my hearing. Consequently, with only a little effort, I was able to hear almost everything that passed between them, despite their low voices.

The gist of the conversation was that D.I. Nelson had spoken with the hospital. They had, he told D.S. Nasir in a not-low-enough voice, confirmed the cause of Robert J. Robertson's death as a stab wound to his neck, which was of no surprise to me and explained a good deal about the amount of blood Alice and Phyl had reported, and that the electronic delivery device had been retrieved from his pocket, which *was* a surprise, as I would have thought they would have found that earlier, whilst the body lay in the cleaning cupboard surrounded by police officers but I suppose they were thinking of other, more pressing matters at the time.

I certainly wasn't eavesdropping as such, as one simply can't help it if one has developed particularly astute hearing in compensation for losing one's eyesight, but I have to admit I did hold my breath as he continued, but I think that was probably more from the anticipated shock of what I guessed was about to follow.

The delivery docket, D.I. Nelson told the Detective Sergeant, had been signed by the recipient of the delivery although I don't know how he'd managed to get into the device when the device was in the hospital morgue with the body or wherever it is that they stash the belongings of those who have been brought in lifeless from a murder scene, but then I supposed they had dispatched an officer to the hospital for such occurrences so perhaps the police force is not so thinly-stretched as the media would have us believe. Now I thought about it, it did seem a little excessive to have quite so many officers on the case but perhaps, what with it being the week before Christmas in a town where nothing much happens as a matter of course, they hadn't much else to be getting on with.

"Who?" the D.S. asked, somewhat economically, and he didn't answer, but after a fraction, she said, "A. Devine," so perhaps someone had taken a photograph of the thing and he was showing it to her. She didn't say anything else except, "Thank you Guv," which would have tickled me as I thought police officers only said 'Guv' in movies, if only I hadn't been too shocked by hearing Alice's name linked to such incriminating evidence to be much tickled by anything.

Alice, you see, is Miss Alice Devine.

Whatever was said next, I confess I paid no heed, as I was digesting the news and running it through my mind to see if there were any possible scenarios that would get poor Alice off the hook.

After a minute or so, the D.S. re-entered the staffroom and I can only suppose I displayed some shock on my face because she said, "Ah. You heard that didn't you, Mrs Smith. I'll make you a cup of tea." Without waiting for my response, she went to the sink, ran some water into the kettle and switched it on.

There followed a short interval whilst the bubbling of the kettle was the only sound in the room, and I imagine we were both thinking about how implausible it was that lovely, ditsy Alice could have stabbed a man and killed him, however unpleasant he had been, although as D.S. Nasir had already said, she has seen most things, in her job, so perhaps she wasn't nearly as upset about it as I was. I suppose one is trained to remain emotionally detached, in the police force.

Once the kettle had clicked itself off to indicate the water was boiled, I said in a small, feeble voice that I supposed they were going to arrest Alice, and the D.S. said it seemed that way and as soon as she'd made my tea she'd have to pop out to find out what was going on in the salon and she'd carry my tea back to my seat and leave me there, and I said, "Not with Alice, though," and she said, "Not with Alice, no," and we fell silent once more.

Chapter Eighteen

We sat in silence for a moment or two, while the kettle burbled and settled and I digested the information about Alice and tried to make sense of it all.

Alice, I thought, had seemed terribly surprised at the discovery of the body in the cupboard, and her astonishment had been quite genuine as far as I could tell. It is extremely difficult for one to feign a faint, as one's instinct is to soften one's fall, and I really didn't think it was quite as clear-cut as all that.

"Would it be helpful," I asked tentatively, "if I were to have a little word with Alice. I had quite forgotten Phyllis had said she was red-eyed and watery, and it may be pertinent to find out whatever was the matter with her in case it sheds any light on the situation. And I'm sure Phyllis can ask Maud whether the coffee stain came out of her blouse, in a perfectly casual way as if she had only just remembered about it. Shall I whisper that suggestion in her ear when you return me to my seat? We know it wouldn't have been coffee, as Maud is a tea drinker, so perhaps Phyl can catch her on the hop, as they say." Of course, I had already set Phyl this exact task, but it didn't hurt to drip that little piece of information into the mind of the detective, especially if it may be of help in getting poor Alice off the hook. Unless of course she *had* committed the crime, as the latest evidence suggested, in which case I supposed I'd have to accept things as they were.

D.S. Nasir took my hand in hers and said, "You have been very helpful, Sally, but I think you can leave the rest to us." She let go of my hand and rattled about by the sink with cups and spoons and whatnots and then a moment later she said, "Here's your tea now, but why don't I bring it through for you instead of leaving you alone in here while I see to things?"

I was relieved to think Phyl was already on the case, as it were, and the plan already set in motion, but also a little disappointed at the detective's insistence that she had everything under control and did not have any further need of our assistance. I had quite relished the thought of doing a spot of undercover detecting to fill the time, but the Detective Sergeant seemed very capable so I supposed she knew what she was doing.

With that, she helped me to my feet and guided me to the door with the same thoughtful attention to directing me as she had given before, which was no mean feat as she was also carrying my hot mug of tea.

"Mind the door frame, there you are, past the toilets. Almost there now."

The scent of pine and Christmas foliage told me we were just about passing the waiting area. As we progressed further from the staffroom and lavatories, the space widened and the light shifted and changed, a low buzz of chatter filling the salon.

D.S. Nasir walked me to my seat, set the cup of tea carefully on the shelf in front of me, and left me to it. A steady thrum of excitement reverberated around the salon but when I sifted through the babble I could no longer pick out Alice's voice, or that of the Detective Inspector.

"Have they taken her already?" I asked into the space around me, uncertain as to whom I may be addressing or indeed if anyone were in the vicinity to hear me.

Beyond the central mirrors, someone was sobbing loudly. By process of location and common sense, I deduced it must be Maud so I got to my feet without asking or awaiting permission and tap-tapped my way around until I reached her side.

"Goodness," I said, as I placed my hand on her shoulder and rubbed gently in the manner in which I would comfort an upset student in my teaching days. "Are you all right, Maud?" Of course, this was a silly and rhetorical platitude and the poor woman was far from all right. One does tend to ask the most useless questions in these circumstances, don't you find?

"She didn't kill him," Maud gasped between sobs.

"Phyllis, dear, has Maud a tissue?" I called to my friend, as I presumed she was still seated where I had left her, just along from poor Maud, and sure enough, just a second later, there was a waft of lily of the valley and Phyllis was beside me, resting a hand on my arm to let me know she was there.

"Here, Maud, have a good blow," Phyl said, ever the practical one in a time of crisis.

"She couldn't have killed him." Maud spluttered and sniffed and had a blow. "She didn't kill him."

My heart was all of a flutter as I imagined how I would react if my granddaughter were in such a position. I suspected I would be just as disbelieving and utter all manner of protests of her innocence, as I simply couldn't imagine her stabbing anyone in the neck and killing them no matter how despicable they may be towards her, even though she has got a frightful temper at times, which she must have got from her father's side of the family, I should think.

I rubbed Maud's back with small circular motions between her shoulder blades, and Phyl must have had one of those nifty packs of pocket tissues as there was a rustle of cellophane and a rustle of tissue and Maud blew again.

"There, there," Phyl said, as one does.

"I'm sure it will all be all right," I said, although to be perfectly honest I felt nothing of the sort but could hardly come out and say, "Well she'll be off to prison for a very long time, won't she?"

"Could I have your attention for a moment please?" The Detective Sergeant's voice carried clearly across the salon and we all fell obediently silent. "We'll just wind up a couple of things here and then you will all be free to go," she said. "I'm sure some of you may need to make arrangements, and P.C. Finbury here will get your phones back to you in just a moment. If anyone has any questions or needs any assistance, just let him know as he comes around to you."

There was another wave of shuffling and chatter in response, and she added something about not discussing the events on social media just yet, but I supposed the afternoon's drama would be announced on the evening news as nothing so exciting usually happens in Little Wittering. I wouldn't be at all surprised if we made the headlines and if there might even be a photographer waiting outside on the pavement so it was a good thing the stylists had been permitted to complete everyone's hairdo and not leave us half-finished. Even when one is unable to see oneself on the television, it must be far more pleasant to have people come up and compliment one's hair rather than whisper behind their hands about what a dreadful fright someone looks. Once I got wind of this notion, I must confess I became quite excited at the thought of being captured by a photographer and Dennis spotting me on the television with my hair freshly set. Not Gordon's Jill from Market Yard, of course, as she doesn't do that kind of work. I imagine the press have their own specialist photographers. They certainly used to but one never knows, with all this modern development.

The Detective Sergeant asked us to all be patient for just another short while but agreed that she supposed it would do no harm for us to talk amongst ourselves before she sent us all home, as we'd no doubt all had quite the shock and it might be good for us to talk about it with others who'd shared the experience.

When she stopped talking, Maud said again that Alice couldn't possibly have done it, and I patted her shoulder and didn't answer, because really, what was there to say?

"You don't understand," she said, with a rather uncouth sniff. "She thought he had left. She didn't know he was still here."

Well, that got my attention, I can tell you.

"What do you mean, Maud?" I said, aware that Phyllis had stiffened beside me and was waiting for the answer with quite as much trepidation as I.

"She let him in, signed for the delivery, and held open the door to the cupboard," Maud said.

Phyllis let out a whoosh of breath. "Why didn't she say? When everyone was asked?"

"Everyone said he hadn't come in," I added.

"He arrived just as we did," Maud said. "Alice was a bit abrupt with the odious man, told him to come back in twenty minutes or so, when the salon would be open and everyone would be back. He laughed at her and said he was busy and she was there now and it would only take a minute and not to be so dramatic." Maud sniffed into the tissue, muffling her words. "I said it wouldn't hurt, would it, and she said oh all right then, and in he came with a box of whatever. Just one box it was, so he hadn't a trolley or anything fancy like that, although he needed both hands for it. Alice said he could dump it in the cupboard out of the way and he asked her to get the door and I went off to have my wee which was the reason we were there and I was afraid I really couldn't wait any longer, and ..." She broke off with a fresh burst of sobbing. "And when I came back out of the loos, he had her pinned up against the counter and was ..." Her tremble ran all up my arms and I lifted my hands from her back for a moment as the feeling was quite unpleasant.

For a moment or two, Maud became quite incoherent and Phyl and I were at a bit of a loss.

Claude sidled over to us as Maud's sobs became louder, and he whispered to me to ask whether she needed anything and could he help at all but I think he was under the impression she was just hysterical about Alice having been taken away so I whispered back to ask him if he could get her a glass of water or perhaps some tea, but that was more about getting him to leave us alone for a few minutes longer. I was afraid Maud might clam up if Claude were there listening, and I had the distinct impression she was on the verge of a rather important revelation, so I wanted her to regain her composure and spit it out.

After a minute or so, Maud's sobs subsided into feeble sniffles and I guessed Phyl had handed her another tissue as she said, "Here you are, Maud," but I suppose it could have been something else.

"Are you saying," I asked, now that Maud was calmer again, "that Robertson had come into the salon when you arrived after your lunch and Alice admitted him to the cleaning cupboard, whereupon he pinned her against the shelving in a compromising position?"

"And that she had to fend him off in an act of self-defence?" added Phyl helpfully.

"But why didn't she say so?" I was almost certain it would be a perfectly understandable justification for a young woman to fight off a lecherous man's unwanted and persistent attention, especially when one is frightened and captured in a cupboard, and an outcome the police would have considered with sympathy had she explained the situation at the first opportunity.

"It ... it ..." Maud was having some difficulty with getting the words out, which brought to mind a memory of a tremulous sixteen-year-old Alice standing before me some years ago, nervously trying to articulate why she had not completed her English project in a timely manner.

Maud sniffed again and made a valiant effort to pull herself together with a stiffening of her back and a deep sigh, and I cast aside thoughts of the teenage Alice and gave Maud my full attention.

"When I disturbed them," she said, "Alice scuttled off to the toilets to sort herself out and by the time I found her there, I told her he was gone." She gave another great heaving sigh. "She had no idea he was ... dead. Not until she found him in the cupboard all over again, after you told her to sort out the smell." Her words took on a sharp tone as if the whole hullaballoo was somehow my fault, and I wasn't having any of that.

"She put on a fine show of surprise," I said in an even tone. "She was terribly convincing and seemed quite distraught and terribly shocked."

"Maud," Phyllis said, "what exactly was it you had just rinsed from your blouse when Sally and I arrived in the salon at one o'clock this afternoon?" In that moment, I knew that Phyllis's little grey cells had worked at lightning speed and that she had put together the pieces of the jigsaw.

"Blood?" I whispered, not wanting to believe it at all, but with a simultaneous glimmer of hope that lovely Alice may not have committed the dastardly deed after all. "Was it *you* who stabbed him, Maud?"

Claude pottered up behind us and said, "More tea ladies," in a most cheerful voice which I supposed was in relief that the matter was over with rather than any great pleasure in having witnessed one of his stylists being carted off in handcuffs.

I didn't bother to mention I already had a perfectly good fresh cup of tea awaiting me on the far side of the mirror, where the D.S. had left it just a few moments ago. It hardly seemed pertinent. *Oh Claude*, I thought to myself as he set down the tea somewhere with a clink and a clatter, *it's not over until the fat lady sings*, and then I chuckled inwardly because I remembered how Phyl always described Maud as being quite plump, and here she was, singing about her part in the crime, so that was quite a light moment in a terribly serious confession, don't you agree? Aloud, I said would he be kind enough to give us a few moments and then inform the lovely Detective Sergeant that I would like to have another little word with her. "She is still here, isn't she?" I added in a brief flutter of panic. I was quite certain Dougal Rufus would exhibit not a single degree of sympathy or kindness towards Maud, nor the patience to hear what she had to say, as he was not the type to seek an alternative outcome once a solution had been reached, whether it be a correct solution or a false one.

"She is," Claude said and my shoulders loosened in relief. "I will walk very slowly towards her for you and cough when I get near her. If you are ready for her, cough back twice. If you are not ready, cough three times."

"Oh, you clever man!" A secret code, what fun! I almost lost my focus in the thrill of it, but a sniff from Maud and a sharp "Ahem!" from Phyllis soon reminded me of the seriousness of the occasion and brought me back to the matter in hand.

"All right, Maud," I said in my very firmest teacher's voice. "Tell us what happened when you returned from the lavatories and discovered your granddaughter trapped in the cupboard with Robertson."

Her body had stilled and her sniffles eased and although her voice shook a little when she began to speak again and I had to lean forward to hear, her words were clear and certain.

"He had his back to me, blocking her from my view, but she cried out to me and I could tell at once she was scared. He had her arms pinned and was leaning over her. They were arguing, and he didn't see me come up behind them. She told him to leave her alone and she wasn't interested in him anymore and she used some very unpleasant words, Sally, very unpleasant, but he didn't let her go, so I tapped him on the back and said what did he think he was doing and he spun around to face me. Alice ducked out from under his arm and scooted off past me into the toilets, crying; her clothes all dishevelled from where he'd pulled at her and she'd tried to get away from him."

"He didn't ..." Phyllis couldn't form the words, but I knew exactly what it was she was wondering as I'd had the same reaction when Maud said about her clothes being dishevelled and we are quite in tune with each other as I think I have mentioned.

Maud must have guessed our thoughts too, because she said, "No, no, I don't think ..." and Phyl and I both breathed a sigh and said, "oh thank goodness," in perfect harmony, which really does show you how similar we are in our ways.

"But goodness knows what might have happened if you hadn't come in," I said with a little shudder, remembering how Flora and Annabel and Alice and Claude and Gordon had all said Robertson had quite the reputation and was exactly the kind of horrible man inclined to make unwanted advances.

"Yes," agreed Maud, "I wouldn't have been a bit surprised." She paused to catch her breath and there was the clink of earthenware on glass and a soft slurp and swallow so she must have picked up the tea Claude had brought us and had a quick swig.

I was just about ready for another cup myself, and wished I'd thought to take a few mouthfuls before coming round to find Maud, but wishes aren't horses, and you'd have thought I'd had quite enough tea by then, given how much of the blessed stuff I'd drunk through the afternoon. Nonetheless, my mouth was dry and I would have welcomed a sip but I wasn't entirely sure where to locate the mug Claude had set down, so I'd have to wait until there was a suitable lull in Maud's accounting of the day's events to ask Phyl to pass it across and place it safely into my hands.

"I'm still not exactly clear how he ended up dead on the floor, so perhaps you could just explain that part?" Dear Phyllis had read my mind once more, as this was the part about which I, too, remained somewhat unclear.

"Alice ran off into the toilet, and I told the man as firmly as I could that he must leave immediately, although I'm afraid my voice wasn't at all steady, I can tell you. He is—was—quite imposing and he was really quite angry and I don't mind telling you I was quite afraid." Her voice trembled a little but after another sip of her tea she rallied nicely and continued quite calmly. "I was afraid he might run after Alice, or push me aside and send me flying, and as he came towards me, I spotted the scissors lying on the countertop under the shelves." She shuddered again and I wondered if she'd added a fresh spill to her blouse.

"You poor thing," Phyllis said softly, which was a terribly generous thing to say to someone in the throes of confessing to having stabbed a man to death, but Phyl is a very kind person so I wasn't at all surprised by her compassion in the moment.

"Oh Phyllis," Maud said so quietly I had to listen very carefully to catch the words, "I ... I simply snatched them up without thinking, and Phyllis, Sally, I ... I'm terribly afraid I jammed them towards him and ... and ..." Her voice became quite croaky and crackly and then completely inaudible, and I suspected she was on the verge of a fresh bout of tears but I think we'd got the gist of it by then and even Dougal Rufus would have been able to join the dots quite successfully, I should think.

I patted Maud on the shoulder again and at just that moment Claude coughed somewhere on the other side of the room and I'd almost forgotten that he was going to alert the Detective Sergeant, what with all the excitement of Maud's revelation, so I couldn't remember how many coughs I was supposed to give in return which rather spoiled the fun of the little code he'd invented.

I coughed once, and then after a little breath, coughed twice in quick succession, then took another little pause, before giving three coughs together, but in case he didn't quite get my meaning, I waved my cane in the air too, although I had to hastily put it down again when Phyllis said, "Ouch, watch it, Salamander," in a most petulant tone.

"Oops-a-daisy," I said. "Sorry, although you do know I—"

"Can't watch it!" Phyl finished for me with a feeble little tinkling giggle so I mustn't have hit her too hard.

"Oh dear, Maud," I said as kindly as I could, "I'm sure they will understand. It sounds to me as if you were acting in a very responsible manner to stop a horrible lecherous pest of a man attacking poor Alice, so I'm sure it won't be as bad as you think." I paused to let that sink in. "Maud, did Alice really not know what you'd done?"

"I told her he had left while she was in the toilets, and I told her to go off and make us a cup of tea for the shock. She was still quite teary, so I suppose that's why she didn't notice I had a little splash of blood on my blouse, or perhaps she just thought I'd spilled my lunch as it wouldn't be the first time ... and I'd stashed the scissors in my handbag ... By the time I'd cleaned myself up ... I had to be quick, you know, so I got out before she was finished with the tea?"

"Yes," Phyllis said agreeably, as if washing a dead man's blood off one's blouse whilst one's granddaughter makes a cup of tea is a perfectly normal occurrence. Perhaps it is, in the types of books she has read.

"I stuck my head into the staffroom, told her he'd gone, and asked if she needed any help with the tea, and she said no, I wasn't allowed in the staffroom and she'd manage. She sounded like she needed a minute to finish pulling herself together—you know how these young ones are? They don't like to get all teary in public—I said all right then, I'd go and make myself comfy in the salon and she wasn't to worry about that awful man anymore, and about half a minute after I'd sat myself down, Claude and Flora came in, and then Gordon and you two, and that was that and I hadn't the time to think about the consequences of what had happened at all after that."

I supposed with Alice's hands full of tea, and the hubbub of everyone arriving back after lunch, Alice hadn't thought to check whether Robertson really had left the premises or whether he might be lying in his own blood, dying in the cleaning cupboard. One really would be forgiven for not thinking that, especially as Maud is not usually the type to go around stabbing people with scissors, as far as I know.

"So she really *was* surprised to find him there in the cupboard." Phyll said softly. "Poor girl."

"And she couldn't say anything as she must have immediately realised that her gran had stabbed him ... she was protecting you by not telling anyone she'd admitted him into the salon, accepted the delivery, and had a conflab with him in the cupboard. The poor girl must have been in a terrible dilemma." No wonder she seemed clumsier than ever as she attended to my hair. I squeezed Maud's shoulder, thinking about poor Alice.

Whilst my hand was still resting on Maud's shoulder, D.S. Nasir approached us in her sensible shoes, put her hand on my arm and said, "I think I can take this from here, thank you Sally. Maud Devine, would you come with me down to the station and we'll see what we can do about getting Alice released." She seemed to have sized up the situation quite well, so I supposed she must have been near enough to hear much of our conversation. "We'll get you settled into an interview room down at the station and ask you a few more questions. Would that be all right?"

I let my hand drop from Maud's shoulder and Maud scooted her chair a fraction away from me, got herself to her feet, and off they went. I fumbled about for the arms of the vacated chair and sank into it. "Phyl, won't you be a dear and put that tea into my hands before it goes cold? I think I could do with a little drink."

Phyl did as I requested, but as she set the hot mug into my grasp, she said quite loudly, "I think we will be free to go very soon, so why don't we go over to the hotel and have a little gin and then I will get you home to Dennis and you won't be so terribly late for your dinner after all."

Chapter Nineteen

I was correct about the newspapers, because not fifteen minutes after Phyllis suggested her little idea about the gin, Finbury said we could leave, although we shouldn't be at all surprised if there was need for some follow-up questions later, and we were all terribly excited about leaving the salon and everyone scrabbled to the door like hyenas at a corpse. Of course, Phyllis and I were more dignified about it all and after Flora and Bobby-Jo and Annabel and Josephine had rushed out just as fast as they could, Phyllis guided me out of the salon at a more sedate pace as befitting of two septuagenarians.

As we crossed the threshold, a waft of icy air lifted my newly-styled hair from my neck and caused a little chill, and there was a click-click and a momentary burst of light and Phyllis said, "Take that camera out of our faces," in a terribly sharp voice, tightening her grip on my arm as she spoke. She tried to lead me onwards, but someone stepped into our path and said they'd heard about the murder in the salon and someone else called out to ask us if could we answer a few questions, which was as I had predicted and I supposed it was the people from the television news as well as the Wittering Chronicle because it seemed as if there was a bit of a crowd.

Phyl stiffened at my side and I couldn't tell if she was a deer caught in headlights or a woman on the verge of divulging everything we'd witnessed, so I nudged her with my elbow, lifted my cane a fraction, and said in my firmest voice that as they could perfectly well imagine, I hadn't seen anything at all, and my friend was escorting me home to recover from the shock so would they would kindly move out of our way?

The owners of the voices moved backwards a little, out of our space, and I think we'd got away with it, but nonetheless, I stood straight and lifted my chin a fraction and held my stance for a moment, just in case anyone might take another photograph.

"Come along, Sal," Phyllis said, and led me off down the street away from it all, and all of a sudden we were just two old friends enjoying a stroll down the high street on the last Thursday before Christmas, albeit away from a hair salon where a murder had taken place and a little old grandmother and her granddaughter had been removed to the police station for questioning.

"We'll cross here," Phyllis said a minute or two later, and as we had just passed the place where the pavement dips to allow vehicle access to the little passage between the Bread and Breakfast and The Leaky Tap, I guessed we had reached the zebra crossing outside the post office. She turned me towards the kerb and we teetered for a moment at the side of the road until the traffic stopped.

Not very many minutes after that, we were stationed quite contentedly in the comfortable lounge of the Little Wittering Hotel, with a gin and tonic in our hands and a fire at our sides.

As I took the first nourishing sips of my gin, Phyllis let out a girlish giggle.

"Don't think I didn't notice you preening for the camera," she said, "but you turned your face quite the wrong way. He'd moved around us to get a snap of Claude, who came out after us! They only let us get away because he was more interesting to them, what with being the owner of the establishment, I should think." She chortled in a most unladylike way and I batted at her with my free hand, but she must have ducked away out of reach, as I swiped nothing but empty space.

Nonetheless, I laughed with her, because overall, it had been a most dramatic afternoon and we were glad of a little light relief.

"I am awfully pleased," I said, when we had regained our composure, "that it wasn't Alice after all."

"Or Claude."

"Or Gordon."

"Me too," Phyl said.

"Poor Maud, though," I said.

"Poor Maud," Phyl agreed.

We were silent for a moment while we sipped our gin and tonics and thought about how we'd have preferred it not to have been anyone, but hopefully the police would be lenient on Maud, who had, after all, been doing what any grandmother would have done in the circumstance of finding their granddaughter being compromised in such a way. At least, I imagine that's what Phyllis was thinking, as I was thinking it, and we are usually quite in tune with each other.

Of course, that's not to say either of us would have actually *killed* the man, and I'm not condoning that, not at all, but

I don't suppose Maud *meant* it to happen, so I'm sure you understand my sentiments on the matter. One does hear of acts of extraordinary strength in unexpected moments of crisis, like that young mother who lifted a Ford Focus off her child's foot a year or so back, so I expect it was a bit like that for Maud too, and no one would ever have thought she'd have had it in her.

I sighed, and so did Phyllis, and then a lovely deep voice said, "Can I get you another one, Ladies? I hear you've had an exciting afternoon. Your hair is looking lovely, though. Good thing it was a hair salon you got stuck in, or who knows what you'd have come out looking like. This one's on the house. Boss said."

"Ooh, Zachary, you darling man," Phyllis said in a terribly flirtatious voice. "That would be wonderful. I am glad we got here in time to see you after all."

He laughed, and off he went to fetch us both another gin.

"Phyllis! You are quite incorrigible! Whatever would Frederick say?"

"He is such a good-looking young man," she said, which didn't answer my question. "I do so wish you could see him."

"Phyllis," I said again, trying to sound stern but unable to hide the amusement in my voice, so I expect she knew I was joking.

Before either of us could say any more, a familiar wet nose pushed itself into my hand, and dear Dennis was there beside me, saying, "Budge up, I've come to rescue you," and Frederick's quavery voice said, "What would I say about what?"

I was terribly surprised to hear them, but I must say it was a most welcome surprise. I took Dennis's dear old familiar hand in mine and told him he mustn't worry and all the excitement was over and he was far too late to rescue us anyway, as according to Phyllis, a dashing young barman already had that in hand.

Dennis laughed but I knew he was still worried because he patted my hand a few times and said, "Dear Sally. My poor darling little Salamander. I was so worried when I heard on the radio that there was an incident in the hair salon and I imagined all kinds of awful things and I am so very glad you are safe. Frederick and I came as soon as we heard. In a taxi, Sal! In a taxi!"

Amity gave a soft little whine as if to say, "I'm here too."

I gave her ears a good rub and told her I was very happy she was here, and she must have deduced all was well, as she turned around, huffed, and sank down onto my feet in front of the fire.

"We rushed straight to the salon," Frederick added, "and that silly little freckle-faced policeman said you'd left and we asked him where you had gone and he said how would he know, he can't be expected to keep tabs on all the residents of the town."

"And I was about to tell him exactly what I thought, but your Claude stepped in and said he'd heard you saying you needed a stiff drink and we'd probably find you here," Dennis said.

"And here you are." Frederick wheezed as he spoke and sounded terribly out of puff, and I had a sudden vision of the two of them charging along the high street with Amity trotting at their heels like characters in a television show, which gave me a terrible fit of giggles for a few minutes.

When I had recovered myself, my stomach gave a little rumble and I thought about what Phyllis had said about not being late for dinner after all, and I said to Dennis, "Did you manage to warm up that Shepherd's pie?"

Dennis didn't answer straight away, and then he said, "About that, Sal…" and tailed off.

I didn't say anything because I was too pleased he had come to find me to be cross with him, but my stomach gave another little rumble and then Frederick had the most marvellous idea, and when Zachary came back with our drinks, Frederick asked him if we could move to a proper table and have a look at the menu, and Zachary said he'd bring the menus over now, and he could get us a table ready in the restaurant in about ten minutes, would that do?

"I'll sort you out just as soon as I can," he said, and then it was Phyllis's turn to get the giggles.

"I suppose he is quite dashing," Frederick said, when she eased up. "He looks very much like I did at twenty-four." Of course, that set Phyl off again, and we'd almost forgotten about poor Maud and the terrible events of the afternoon, when we were interrupted by the squeaking of shoes on the floor, a reek of Marlboro, and a groan from Phyllis, and the moment was ruined.

"Mrs Smith," Finbury said, close enough that his body odour wafted up and smacked me in the nostrils, "I've been dispatched by the D.S. to bring you this." He leaned further into my personal space and shoved something into my hands.

"Your scarf," Phyl said, helpfully, although I'd recognised its silky fabric and scent. I buried my nose into it at once, in the hope it may provide a barricade to the whiff of Finbury.

"You left it in the salon," Finbury added, which even an imbecile could have deduced, so it was no great endorsement of his policing skills. "I'm also to tell you Alice will face some charges for hindering our enquiries, but the D.S. said I must be sure to tell you that she will almost certainly get off lightly. She thinks although Maud is in some trouble, they will take the circumstances into account. She said I should be let you know you were a help." He sounded as if he might be speaking through gritted teeth, but then he added, "Well done, Mrs Smith," in quite a convincing manner, so perhaps he might turn out to be a reasonable enough constable, in time.

"Thank you, Dougal," I said, lowering the scarf from my face, and then there was a squeal, a yelp, a whimper, and a crash.

Dougal Rufus swore in a manner most unsuited to a police constable, so I may have been correct in my initial assessments of his capabilities after all. "Is that dog *supposed* to be in here?" he said.

Beside me, Dennis shuffled to his feet. "I'll walk you out, Dougal Finbury," he said, in the calm, no-nonsense manner one might expect from a retired army officer even though Dennis was a milkman before he retired and has always been a pacifist. "Good girl, Amity. Lie down and look after Sal for me."

While Dennis escorted Finbury from the premises, Frederick produced Amity's guide dog harness, which the two men had thoughtfully swept up in their chivalrous dash to rescue us, and helped me fasten it around Amity's soft midriff. I felt a little sorry for Amity at the necessity of putting her into her harness, as with Dennis and Phyllis at my side, she could quite easily have remained a dog 'at ease' and relaxed in front of the fire, but at least it would alleviate any further discussion as to her presence in the hotel, even though she is quite the regular, and the staff know her well.

By the time Dennis returned, Amity was 'on guard' and Zachary had readied our table, so I allowed Amity to guide me, in order to let her think I needed her, and as soon as we sat, I relaxed her harness once more and slipped her a little dog treat from my handbag, after which she curled up under the table, rested her head on my foot, and began to snore softly.

After a short conflab, I ordered a nice chicken curry, Phyllis chose the salmon, and Frederick said he'd have the steak please.

"And I'll have the shepherd's pie, I think," Dennis said, which told me all I needed to know about the M&S microwaving attempt.

Somewhere outside the windows, the first notes of Silent Night drifted towards us. Phyllis said something about the carol singers being out, and wasn't it lovely, and I allowed myself to imagine gently swirling flakes of snow, which is a benefit of being unable to see the grey drizzle Dennis told me about later. The chatter of the restaurant and the tantalising aromas of our freshly-cooked meals drifted around us, and Little Wittering settled back into its usual state of quiet calm, where nothing very eventful happens.

Acknowledgements

As ever, the biggest thanks are to you. Thank you for reading my book(s). I'd probably keep writing even if you didn't read them, but it's so much more rewarding when I know they get read!

I hope you enjoyed getting to know Mrs Sally Smith as much as I did. Like Sally Smith, my paternal grandmother became blind in adulthood, due to diabetic glaucoma, not long before I was born. I only have a handful of memories of her, as she died when I was very young, but she brushed my hair more gently than anyone (and I had very tangly hair). I would sit in her dim basement kitchen, and she would gently, so gently, unknot my tangles with her fingers and a red Mason Pearson hairbrush. I also have a vivid snapshot memory of walking along a road with her and her guide dog, Amber, although I have no idea where we had been or where we were going.

Amber lived on for several years after grandma died, with first my grandfather and then my aunt, and I remember her with far more clarity than I remember either of my grandparents. Writing Mrs Smith has reminded me of them all, and has had me poring over pictures of the two grandparents I hardly had time to know, and quizzing my dad and my aunt on long-forgotten memories of their mother. I've felt a sadness over not knowing her that I hadn't really considered before, but also an incredible pleasure in writing this book, as, by putting myself in my grandma's shoes as I navigate Mrs Smith's world I feel I've got to know my grandma better.

So, thank you to my mum, dad, and aunt, who found photos of my grandparents and Amber, and put up with my questions about them. (And then got sucked into the rabbit hole of trying to work out who else was in the photos. Sorry!) My aunt might also recognise elements of herself in Mrs Smith, not least in name.

I also, as always, thank my husband for his ongoing support, and my children, who are finally beginning to read my books now they've realised other people actually read them.

Thank you Shayne, cover-designer-become-friend, who planted the seed for Mrs Smith to start with. She can be found at www.WickedGoodBookCovers.com.

Thank you to my son's friend Eilidh, who took EXACTLY what I had in my mind for the character portraits and drew them. She can be found at www.instagram.com/aileemarie_art.

Thank you to my earliest readers: authors Kelly Young, Louise Finch, and Jay Larkin; loyal reader Cindy; new reader Jill, and my wonderful audio narrator Helen Lloyd. Your encouragement and comments have been wonderful. An especially massive thank you to Helen for 'sorting out' the audio book. 'Wow!' and 'Thank you!' don't go anywhere close to summing **that** up!

I can't wait to write the next mystery for Mrs Smith to solve! I promise Amity will feature more in the next one.

About the Author

For up-to-date news and exclusive content including maps, images, and extra stories about the characters in Jinny's cozy mystery series, please sign up for Jinny's newsletter by popping over to her website and choosing one of the free short stories listed there:

www.jinnyalexander.com

Say hello at facebook.com/JinnyAlexanderAuthor

or

instagram.com/jinnyalexanderauthor/

If you enjoyed the book, please take a moment to leave a review on Amazon and Goodreads. Thank you.

Jinny was first published in Horse and Pony magazine at the age of ten. She's striving to achieve equal accolades now she's (allegedly) a grown-up. Jinny has had some publishing success with short story and flash competitions and has been long-listed for the prestigious Bath Flash Fiction Award, placed second in Flash 500, and has been published in MsLexia Magazine and Writing Magazine, among other publishing credits. Jinny has recently completed an MA in Creative Writing with the University of Hull, for which she was awarded a Distinction.

Jinny is the author of the Jess O'Malley Irish Village Mystery Series, the Mrs Smith's Suspects cosy mystery series, and a handful of standalone novels.

Jinny also teaches English as a foreign language to people all over the world and finds her students a constant source of inspiration for both life and stories. Her home, for now, is in rural Ireland, which she shares with her husband and far too many animals. Her two children have grown and flown, but return across the Irish Sea when they can.

Also by Jinny Alexander

The Jess O'Malley Irish Village Mystery Series

The fourth and fifth Jess O'Malley mysteries, *A Deathbed of Roses* and *A Snapshot of Murder*, will be coming soon.

Jinny is currently working on more sequels to both series.

Jinny also has stories and flash fiction in anthologies and magazines. A more comprehensive list can be found on her website at www.jinnyalexander.com

Dear Isobel (March 2022, Creative James Media) is currently out of print following Jinny's reversion of rights.

Praise for *A Diet of Death*

This is a light-hearted cosy that will delight fans of
M C Beaton's Agatha Raisin. […] Highly
recommend it to those looking for a frothy,
enjoyable read that is low on violence and high on
feel-good entertainment!

MAIRI CHONG,
The Dr. Cathy Moreland Mysteries

Well-written and intriguing, this mystery
revolving around members of a weight-loss
group is one that will keep you turning the
pages until the very end.

KELLY YOUNG,
The Travel Writer Cozy Mystery Series

A classic British style whodunnit.
With an engaging and believable heroine - Jess O'Malley - and
set in rural Ireland, this is a fun mystery with lots of heart.
An enjoyable read leading to a satisfying solution, already
looking forward to the next book.

GERALDINE MOORKENS BYRNE
The Caroline Jordan Mystery series and *On
the Fiddle! The Music Shop Mysteries*

The whole book was a warm, comforting read for
anyone who loves mysteries. Highly suggested for
fans of *The Thursday Murder Club*.

ALISON WEATHERBY,
The Secrets Act

Jinny Alexander's outstanding cosy mystery
A Diet Of Death is a real treat.
(And not the kind with calories!)

J. IVANEL JOHNSON,
The JUST (e)STATE Cozy Mysteries

This tale is a homage to those much loved
classic detective authors, and is perfect for
escaping the worries and stresses of the world.

LOUISE MORRISH,
Operation Moonlight

Jinny Alexander embeds her murder mystery with the satisfying
atmosphere of rural Ireland. […] Cozy mystery readers who enjoy stories
of friendships and murder possibilities will find *A Diet of Death* unusually
strong in its atmosphere, which does equal justice to both the murder
mystery component and the entwined lives of a small village […]

MIDWEST BOOK REVIEW

Made in United States
Orlando, FL
24 February 2025

58861666R00135